Jane Burdiak lives in Buckinghamshire and is married with four sons. On completion of her fashion degree in 1972 she began working as a designer and in 1976 opened her own business, designing and making clothes to order. Then, fifteen years later changed direction and became a teacher. Since then Jane has been teaching textiles and food technology and enjoys the challenge of a demanding and stimulating environment. She began writing two years ago and has recently completed her first book.

PATCHWORK

Jane Burdiak

PATCHWORK

To Simon and Lucy
from
Jane Burdiak.

AUSTIN & MACAULEY

As far as the author is aware, all of the events in Patchwork are
based on true facts. Some names have been changed so as not to
offend. The author does not accept responsibility for anything
written about the characters that other people may see as
themselves.

A CIP catalogue record for this title is
available from the British Library.

ISBN 978 1 905609 45-1

www.austinmacauley.com

First Published (2009)
Austin & Macauley Publishers Ltd.
25 Canada Square
Canary Wharf
London
E14 5LB

Printed & Bound in Great Britain

DEDICATION

For Anne More Nicholson

ACKNOWLEDGEMENTS

Special thanks to my friend who sat beside me in the car all the way to Scotland, twice; to my brothers and sisters that I didn't know I had; to my two sons who installed the ink cartridges in the printer and taught me how to email; to my husband who is always there; to Linda Nelson at The Army Personnel Centre in Glasgow for digging up the past; to Maggie at Abbott's Hill School for showing me around; to Daphne Lakin for her lasting wartime memories and above all to Elaine, to whom I am truly indebted for her technical expertise.

Also

Cargoes and Sea Fever by John Masefield

The Owl and the Pussycat by Edward Lear

Prayer by Mary L Duncan

And

One line from 'Hey Joe' by Jimi Hendrix
One line from 'The Broad Majestic Shannon' by the Pogues

She never wore the hat. Well, not on that occasion. She placed it carefully on her pillow in the back of the stuffy car. She had carried it into her room three weeks earlier, expecting to wear it dreamily, or to create a darkness in the white light or to hide her crying eyes.

Her room, which she shared with her husband, was sparsely furnished. The hat was stored in the dark on the top shelf of the wardrobe. Green shutters prevented the heat from penetrating the room and a wooden roller blind filtered out the sun. Out of habit and the need for light, she rolled up the blind and tied the cord in a clumsy bow. She pushed open the warm shutters to reveal a small balcony, only wide enough to stand and call to people in the street below. The railing was hot to touch. She looked left and right. The houses seemed to have four levels. In many, the top floor was open without shutters or blinds and in the house opposite a line of washing was motionless, evaporating quietly in the dark hot space. It was the only sign of habitation. Windows stared blankly back, shutters firmly down, their peeling green paintwork dulled and blistered. Cables and wires criss-crossed the narrow street, delivering messages, gossip and news. The rough textured walls had seen better days. The tired, worn colours, faded and loved by travellers from Europe. The hefty doors opened directly onto the pavement, just recessed in slightly. The doors, especially the wide ones, were all slightly different. The pavements were narrow and the road *Carrer Iglesia* was only wide enough for one vehicle. From the balcony the road sloped down to the right to *Carrer Seguer*. This was the view.

She sat on the bed near the window. Her bed. She felt uneasy and restless. She could hear people talking clearly as though they were next to her. She stood up. Dusty panelled windows were fastened back. She tried closing them but found the dark, airless, stifling atmosphere, unbearable. She returned the window arrangement to its original form, realizing that having some air was better than none at all. Despite the strong sunlight, a light suspended from the ceiling threatened the gloom. There were two single beds, metal framed beds with brown striped polyester duvets. Nothing romantic here and nothing feminine either, not even cotton. The pillows, like trifle sponges, were mean and had a mind of their own. A lamp sat on a flat pack set of drawers, between the two beds. Two rattan chairs added charm, but soon became buried under discarded clothes.

She didn't unpack. She lived, the entire three weeks, out of her holdall. This was not like her. Whether the look was Bohemian or County, her clothes were clean, pressed and ready to go. To her, there was simply nowhere to put them, nowhere that was special for her things. She would have made do with a picture rail, but there wasn't one. At least her bag was her own. There was truly nothing wrong with the wardrobe. The whole situation seemed hopeless.

She could remember a time when she was in hospital and became totally unreasonable about a moquette chair that sat beside her bed. She could not bring herself to sit in it nor could she ask for it to be removed. In fact, it was not important at all, almost incidental but it seemed so important to her. How could this usually level headed woman have such absurd ideas? Her big, fat bag sat on the floor. It occupied the space between one of the rattan chairs and the door, dumped as though she could have carried it no further and had to deposit it at the earliest opportunity. She moved it in short, quick bursts, both hands round the handles, held in front of her like a bucket of coal. She had felt pleased as she zipped it up, not forced but a tension, still room for something else. It was indeed heavy and the canvas moulded itself around the folded piles that forty eight hours earlier had sat on her bed at home waiting to be transported. Awkward shapes pushed against the grain. Two strong zips gripped her world together. The contents were chosen carefully, for comfort and colour. For you got more wear out of your clothes if you mixed and matched.

There was nothing horribly bright, no red, no pink. There were her linen trousers in khaki and chocolate and a cotton skirt in khaki and a pair of long shorts that had once belonged to her son, also in khaki and some tee shirts and vests which matched or contrasted, but went, depending. There were some 'nice' clothes too. A long floaty dress, perfect for relaxing in. The heat of the day gone, sweat showered away, warm sunned skin, heaven. She had worn this particular dress in Florence the summer before. She had been in search of the golden doors. Her friend had seen the doors in the 60's when her then boyfriend Bill and she had toured all over Europe in an old MG. Janet's camera had become confused and taken several pictures on top of one another, including the one of the golden doors. The doors were exquisite, and beside the doors, there was her friend in a soft blue voile dress sprigged with white and azure. She sent the photo to Janet. Clothes were intensely personal. They didn't have to be expensive or designer label but they created a look that was unique to her. She simply never looked like anybody else.

She rarely went shopping for clothes. If she did, she was often disappointed. She preferred to look, without commitment and this might take several hours but it guarded against a poor decision or an irrational choice. She would mull over the clothes she had seen and return. If by chance someone else had her taste, then her philosophy was that she wasn't meant to have it or she would kid herself that it wasn't even there. She was strong minded and seldom lapsed. She would say to herself that the clothes in

15

her wardrobe were better, therefore no need to buy. Certain criteria limited this theory. She had a weakness for interesting fabrics and unusual prints. Price was a factor; she couldn't make shoes or knitwear so a purchase was justified. In other clothes, however, she was looking for a fair price. She knew all about the rag trade and knew the massive mark up that the retailer felt they could pass to their customers. The blue silk dress in her bag, carefully folded to avoid creasing, was a fair price. It was half price. It had been reduced to fifty pounds and she had to try it on. The feel was heavenly. The jacquard chrysanthemums scattered over a plain of thick blue. It was tight around the hem and impossible to walk, but she would soon fix that. It was her first silk dress and the feel of being felt in it was sensual pleasure. She understood now why silk lingerie, although expensive, was such a turn on. Never mind sensible, silk had to be the way forward. She wore this indulgence with a fringe of blue beads given to her by her sister. It sat in the plain boat neckline and from a distance looked as though it was attached to the dress.

She was a natural girl. She had always liked the feel of natural fibres; they made her feel more comfortable about the world, like being organic. She frowned on the man-made fabrics, the by-products of the chemical industry. In recent years, technology had forced her to look at these fabrics in a new light. They had become increasingly varied in texture and have qualities equal to those natural breathing fibres. Marvellous, easy-care, non-iron, dirt-resistant, crease-resistant, anti-static, with stretch. But not traditional, not plain old-fashioned. She ironed like her grandmother. Her mother had told her that one day when she had watched her daughter plough through a basket of ironing. She would iron everything on the wrong side first, the seams, the plackets, the labels, pressing them firmly into position before she did the right side. The iron followed the grain, no pulling or stretching. It was always a task, getting ready for summer, but once complete her satisfaction soon outweighed the labour. The winter clothes just went to the dry cleaners. The bag was full of cotton and linen and for those special moments, the feel of silk. No wool; it was far too hot for wool. Wool belonged to the northern hemisphere and high altitudes. She carried a small travelling iron. It had its own draw-string bag and went on every holiday. Although she had never used it, somehow it was always there to iron out life's wrinkles. Not thinking that she would need pyjamas, she only took one pair. That was a bit of a mistake.

The two beds, marked out as his and hers, were basic. Whenever possible, she and her husband always took their own pillows, never being entirely sure what comfort lay ahead. Being familiar with your pillow promised a peaceful night. The fat cotton-covered pillows sat on top of the thin cream wafers.

When she saw the two beds she had mixed feelings. She was mainly disappointed. There would be no balmy nights, alternating between sweating and showering. Drip drying, feeling cool for a few moments until the moisture exuded once again. Bodies folded and locked into one until sleep consumed. She especially loved in England, the summer evenings and going to bed early. Lying there, when it was still light, the yellow bedroom curtains open to reveal the sky. From her bed she could see the roofs of the houses opposite, and behind them, the poplar trees. She could see the phone wires that fanned out from the branchless tree. Familiar sounds broke into the quiet night air, the cars going too fast down her road, the birds, people's voices. People not yet tired of the day. She would lie on her big wide bed, with the big window open, the evening air cool, her head on the same pillow that now sat on the narrow single bed. She could, however sleep undisturbed in her own private world. During the night she always had a wakeful time. Initially, she would sleep, whether induced by alcohol or sheer tiredness. Then after only a few hours, she would be awake, refreshed. She was never bored. She used this dark, still time to think, to plan, to remember. Her memory darted from one thing to another until it all became a mishmash, a confusion, a muddle that had no shape or logic. She became restless and longed for sleep to escape her whirling mind.

***

When she was away, the luxury of time allowed her to read. At home, she would never read in bed; she found it too uncomfortable. Beside her bed at home there was a small wicker table. It had been purchased at least thirty years ago in a local junk shop. For a long time it had sat in the hall, not with any particular purpose, but it fitted neatly into the recess by the front door, brought about by having an extension. It did, in fact, sit where the outside had been. On the lower shelf there was a dish in the shape of a carved wooden apple bought in Slovenia at a local market. On it there was an arrangement of fir cones, gathered on a trip to the R.H.S. garden in Surrey. A houseplant sat on the table. It never looked healthy. It was called a ficus benjamina, otherwise known as a weeping fig. And how it did weep; it shed dry green leaves daily in spite of being watered and dusted every now and then. She never claimed to be good with houseplants. They needed a steady temperature of twelve degrees centigrade, preferably thirteen, That must have been the problem. It simply froze to death. She grew fed up with the table in the hall. There had been a fire and furniture had got moved about. The table had found itself beside her bed, just the right amount of space. She bought an embroidered napkin which she set at a jaunty angle. It was a lovely buttery yellow, to match the wallpaper. On top of that sat a white crocheted doily, bought on holiday, but she could not remember where. There was a lamp, which she liked. It came from Marks and Spencers, when they first started doing furnishings. It had an Art Nouveau look in glass and brass. She didn't use the lamp; her husband didn't like its bright, clear light. The only other thing on the small table was the clock. It was a cheap plastic clock from the jewellers in the town. The clock was always set for approximately quarter to six. All she did was to move the snib up before she got into bed. In the morning she would move the snib down long before quarter to six, she was always awake, waiting to get up.

The plastic clock sat on the flat pack drawers. There was room for little else, apart from the lamp. It had been reset for an hour later. It was a small rectangular shape, with a white oval face. It was a smoky blue colour, the same colour as the cutlery storage compartment in the kitchen drawer and it had a little cupboard for the battery. The numbers one to twelve were all there. A thin strip of fluorescent green was sandwiched in the hands. The second hand was thin and alert and at night time you could hear its soft, regular tap. The clock before this one was much bigger and although it was a better clock it was not so discreet. When she was away on holiday once, she left her husband to his own devices. He managed to break the multi-purpose dial at the back, rendering it useless. She hadn't liked the clock, not that she particularly liked this one. Clocks for her were really there as a safeguard, just in case she overslept, but she had never known that to happen. When she woke up during the night she would stare at the clock and check the position of the two fluorescent strips in the dark then calculate how many hours it was till she could get up. Occasionally, she would say to her husband in the morning, "I slept all night," as though it was rare, like a mother would comment on her baby going through the night. She always found excuses for her wakefulness. In recent years she had put it down to her job and before that it was because she was poorly and before that it was because of her children, so it was really about thirty years since she had had a good night's sleep. She knew when she looked at the single bed, along with the close, airless heat and the intrusion of the street below she would not be saying, "I slept all night," this holiday.

On the floor between the bed and the drawers was her spongebag. This treasure trove contained all the essentials and more for the foreseeable future. Due to her thriftiness she had restored the lining with a carrier bag. She neatly cut the bag to size, turned in the edge and hemmed it in position. That, she thought, would certainly extend its life for another few months. Most of the contents of the spongebag went into the very inadequate bathroom, hurriedly being finished as they had arrived. Talcum powder, shampoo, deodorant, and all the usual things that sat on the shelf at home, sat on the floor. The toothpaste and brushes sat beside the taps of the sink. The soap too, competed for a place by the taps, but it continually slipped into the sink. There was no mirror in the bathroom. She could not stare back at herself and check her hair or smile and check her teeth. She did have a small mirror in the spongebag. It was a slim, pearly, plastic mirror and opened to show two reflections, one was square and the image returned was hers, the other was round and brought her face closer than she liked. Not only could you see the lines fanning out from the corners of her eyes but you could also see how they dropped into crevices. In recent years she had decided that she did not need to see the invading lines and streaks of white peppering her hair. It was a good thing that eyes too began to grow old and that they, in normal conditions didn't notice the faults that were occurring. Zooming in, she realised that the freckles were not freckles at all; they were liver spots and the coarse facial hair that coiled out of the moles on her chin needed constant attention. Thus the tweezers and other remedies lurked in the spongebag.

The bag of conjuring tricks was there to patch up, mend or disguise her dry and damaged life and if these magic tricks were applied daily, would prevent tomorrow's

20

wrinkles, or today's fine lines. The advanced systems of the spongebag claimed to reduce ageing. The rich formulations which had been clinically tested could revive and revitalize and needed to be applied generously. These intensive treatments could be rolled on, spread on, rubbed in, sprayed on, dispensed or stuck, to protect and relieve life's daily symptoms, assuring her of feeling refreshed and energised, soft and smooth, hair free and carefree. The contents of her make-up bag were minimal, just a couple of long lasting lipsticks, one called Velvet Kiss to wear with blues and whites and one called Under the Sun, which indeed she was, to wear with her muddy colours. It was the one time that she did not need to see her fair eyebrows and eye lashes. She had had them tinted by Lisa a few days before the holiday and although it had nipped at the time, she hadn't said. It was worth the pain and discomfort and just as well in the end because there was no mirror to reflect the correct positioning. Ever since she was twelve or thirteen she had decided that she didn't like her fair brows and lashes; it was comparable to a picture without a frame. Since then she had always drawn them in a thin bow in barely black or charcoal, much the same really. She didn't go anywhere without the eyebrow pencil; it was an essential.

This tinting business was a little luxury that she afforded before a holiday. It gave her a freedom from her daily routine. She lay there, fully clothed on a narrow bed, her head slightly elevated. The room was cool and classical music played quietly in the background, relaxing and soothing the day away. The thick white towels on the bed were covered with a giant toilet tissue, dispensed from a roll on the floor. She wasn't keen on this. Disposable paper was functional, not luxurious; however, nor would she have liked the thought of someone else lying down before her on the thick white towels That was on a par with the moquette covered chair beside her bed in the hospital when she had become really agitated and cried about it over the phone to her sister. The sash window was open a few inches, letting in the sounds from outside. They seemed distant, she had felt removed from the world outside. For her, frequenting a 'lifestyle' experience was not real. The beauty parlour, as they used to be known was upstairs above the hairdresser's. She did not have her hair cut here; it was too expensive. Having her hair cut happened three times a year, out of necessity, if it had become dry and brittle, or too heavy or just plain annoying. Although her hair was long, she never thought of it as being so. Somehow hairdressers never styled her hair how she liked it. Lee, who cut her hair along the road from the life changing experience, knew that she only wanted her hair well cut. He was tall and she needed to stand up to have it cut, so that it wasn't so back breaking for him.

Sometimes she needed assurance and would say 'My hair does not look like that woman's over there,' seeing a woman outside, reflected in her mirror.

'No,' he would say, 'Your hair doesn't look like that.'

She would say, 'I would have it all cut off, if it did.'

That's about all they would say. She couldn't be bothered with hairdresser chat and he probably couldn't either.

Her hair was thick and heavy and still reasonably bright and shiny in spite of the encroaching white wisps. The new white hair was fine, not like her own hair. What she wanted to know was how it grew so long without her noticing or did a strand just lose its colour. If she saw a white hair she would trace it back to its root and pull it out. On each side of her temple she had a white flash and threatened many times to cut herself a feathery fringe. Her husband didn't like the idea, so the badger look remained. She wore it loose and clipped back with two sturdy hair slides. She didn't like it tame and flat to her head as currently was the fashion, but grabbed back and full, wild and full of movement. She didn't mind if the air was damp or she got caught in the drizzle, it made her hair even more voluminous. Clean hair whispered softly to her as she moved her head. Only the other day a boy waiting to escape from her classroom at half past three touched her hair, it was as though he couldn't help it; he had a look on his face. She had to say something but he meant no harm, no more than if she touched a new born baby, touching gently with the back of her index finger the soft downy newborn skin or stroking an arm softer than a peach. It was impossible not to. Her children, when they were small, took it upon themselves to mess about with her hair. Like primates they would sit behind her in the big armchair and look for nits, totally absorbed, watching the hair move this way and that, dark and light, lifting it up and letting it drop, their little hands getting tangled. Her hair framed her face and was important to her. She went to great lengths when first at secondary school to style it on big rollers. There were jumbos with plastic teeth and large springs covered with brown plastic mesh and a sprig of bristle which always tried to get out. They were fastened in place with a hairpin or a Kirby grip or they had a plastic clip that slotted over the whole roller. So determined was she for the desired effect in the morning, she would sleep in them all night. She would even wear them out with a head square folded and tied at the nape of her neck, the twelve lumps smoothed in the bias of the cloth. In the paper recently she had seen a celebrity with the very same look, thinking it was new and cool to go out in your rollers with a scarf on, trend setting, as though it had never been done before. Her hair rolled under smoothly in the perfect bob. In assemblies she used to hide behind her hair when everyone was praying, with her eyes wide open. 'You vain creature,' her form teacher would say when he caught her brushing her hair behind the lid of her desk, or, 'Your ears are not meant for hooks.'

It was darker in those days, her mother called it auburn; peers at school made fun and called her ginger. She felt hurt by the comments, but put up with them stoically, if she had said anything, nobody would have been interested anyway. No bullying box in those days. When she was small she wore her hair in two plaits just slightly behind her ears or one thick plait down her back. She stood perfectly still in the same place, at right angles to the kitchen sink, her arms down by her sides, her head slightly forward, quietly uncomplaining. The hair was brushed and combed with vengeance and she remembered the comb slicing into her scalp for a clean continuous line between her forehead and her nape. It was then vigorously divided and pulled into sections, each seized and held firm, then grasped and pulled in jerks until the plait was complete. Her scalp felt tender as the hair was strained and stretched. The plaits were firm and hard and tied tightly with ribbons. She didn't ever remember her hair loose, free to blow in the wind, or brush her face; not even a strand escaped the tyranny. Her sister did not have to endure the same oppression; her hair had a natural curl and was allowed its freedom. She remembered once, going to bed, her rippled hair released from its tension, splayed out, reaching out all over the pillow. She thought that she must look beautiful, like the daughter of a wealthy family in a film, when the mother, and the father too, go in to say, "Goodnight darling," and stand at the bedroom door looking romantic and longing. No one went in to say, "Goodnight darling."

Then, when she was ten it was cut off, so short that she looked like a boy. There was no consultation, no discussion. She was taken to the hairdresser's one Saturday morning and it was felled in a single plait. She was mortified; the hair was collected up and put in a bag to take home. She vowed that never again would her hair be that short. It was only when she was in her thirties that it had to be severely cut to get rid of a perm that had seen better days and since then it had been in various stages of long. She had never had it dyed or highlighted. Complete strangers would comment as though amazed at the colour, intrigued that it hadn't come out of a bottle or that someone her age should have long hair. Sometimes she liked the idea of a short spiky style and using all the new glues and gels available to keep it fixed but her children liked their mum as she was and so the hair had remained, untamed. She knew that as soon as she didn't like the reflection Lee would cut it off and style it, like so many before her. She would look ordinary, domesticated, predictable, and while there was nothing wrong with these qualities she did not see herself like that. She was different, unconventional.

***

Their impending holiday was to be different and unconventional. The town was quiet and desolate as they had driven in, the roads dry and dusty and the silence eerie. She had put it down to being siesta time, time to chill and recharge the batteries ready for the next half of the day. Shutters were down and doors closed. The bar in *el centro* of town near *la iglesia* was *abierto*. What a surprise. Vivid red Estrella Damm plastic chairs and tables spilled onto the street. It was conveniently placed for them and it was shady. There were a few customers having a drink, a chat and a cigarette. She got the euro purse out and paid for *dos cervesa* in a foreign tongue, ninety nine point nine percent English, point one percent Spanish. The beer was ice cold and so needed. They talked in confused uncertainty. They had gone to fish the mighty River Ebro, which starts its epic journey in the Pyrenees and ends in the Mediterranean Sea in the famous rice growing region of Spain. Her husband had come across the holiday during the cold winter months in between hugging the fire and watching television. The advertisement in the magazine was inviting, it seemed like a sound enterprise and so he decided to risk all with a phone call. After a few days it was set in motion and booked. The article read well, good fishing and a full English breakfast. What else could be needed? She needed a lot more and in spite of her, in for a penny, in for a pound spirit, it really knocked the stuffing out of her, that long, long journey ending like that. Tears had filled her eyes. Her husband would have turned round there and then and driven straight home again. She knew he would too. He had this inner strength and sheer determination and he would have driven the thousand miles in one go as though it was just round the corner, but that would have been a failure on her part and she couldn't have that. No, it could not be that bad. True enough, it was not that bad, but it was not that good either, not for her anyway. The men who ran the business were charming, friendly and polite and enjoyed fishing banter, sport, food and general gossip. They had had enough of England and had decided to move to Spain and do their own thing. They had settled into the lifestyle and would not return. She thought that the whole thing needed a woman's touch. The men would have benefited from a woman's touch.

The alcohol had relaxed and blurred their senses as they left their new local. For what, she did not know. The excitement and anticipation of her husband was uncontrollable, and she left him with his new-found friends to escape and explore the town, an excuse really to be on her own. Once again tears filled her eyes as she walked the narrow streets, her sunglasses concealing her sadness. No-one could tell how lonely and desolate she felt. Just a few hours earlier she too had been excited and full of expectation. She sat on a seat in *la placa*, the glaring white light vicious and bright, and although she tried reading her book, she was unable to concentrate. Her mind kept wandering; it became a confused jumble, not knowing in the end what she expected. There was no one around, just mad dogs. Thin, emaciated dogs, just pacing around, sometimes flopping down in a black shady corner or quenching their thirst in the water fountain. Cautiously she moved away. She was not keen on dogs that she was not familiar with and continued through the maze of narrow shady streets churning over the confusion in her head.

She did go on holiday when she was a child. There were the long painful journeys to Scotland to visit relations, taking The Great North Road and usually travelling at night, rarely stopping to stretch or spend a penny. The back of the car was transformed into a small bed for her sister and herself and they lay dovetailed for the entire journey. She remembered the darkness, lying, watching the clouds shaping themselves, hiding the moon, then letting its brightness fill her world, headlights stretching long beams catching the sheep at the side of the road, slumped and looking dead. She hoped they were not. Shadows dark and contorted reaching into unfathomable depths. The black lorries, heavy and labouring, their tarpaulins parcelled and tightly lashed, but sometimes escaping, free to flap and dance, ropes adrift, whipping and punishing. The pink dawn light, not seen before, fused in mist. Sometimes tired raised voices disturbed her dreams when her mother had missed the sign and they had become lost. Never being entirely sure, when waiting for the ferry at Queensferry, that the car would manage the ramp between the land and the sea, that fantastic feat of engineering spanning the Firth of Forth. And arriving, cold and tired.

For her mother it was a busman's holiday, doing much the same but with hard earned savings to spend on luxuries, like fresh floury rolls from the bakery every morning and punnets of raspberries and strawberries and copious amounts of thick double cream. They used to go for afternoon tea at the Victoria Café for her sister's birthday. Cakes were neatly arranged on a three tiered plate stand and there was a birthday cake and it was a highlight of the holiday and cost a lot of money. Her sister was a starlet who could recite poetry and knew Peter Rabbit from cover to cover. All she could manage was a four line stanza. Of course she was envious, although she hadn't known that then. Holidays like those taken in Scotland and camping in Wales were a time of being nice. The daily fighting and arguing ceased and her parents were almost pleasant and behaved like other parents with children in tow, except to her it seemed false, a pretence, a lie, not how it really was.

Once they stayed at Ogmor-by-the-Sea and went to visit some peopled who had camped next to them. Their house was in the Rhonda Valley and backed onto the canal; there was a green spiky guard to deter people from falling into the black water. The evidence of mining was everywhere, the blackness and dreariness leached into the poor drab view. It was damp and drizzly, the air heavy and still. She imagined her white blouse with dainty blue embroidery round the collar speckled with smuts. It was a terraced house, very small, far too small for visitors. They were offered dog food sandwiches, handed round on a plate. They had to stand round a square table because there weren't enough chairs. She knew that her mother would not have approved, but was far too polite to say anything. They went to Porthcawl to a fair. She wouldn't have approved of that either. She and her sister had been treated to a candy floss and watched the man spin the pink sugar, twisting it onto a wooden stick. It was difficult to eat, especially walking along and had to be held at arm's length. She couldn't have been paying attention because her pink candy floss had become detached from its wooden stick and attached itself to a man's overcoat. The man strolled on, unaware. In Snowdon's looming grey shadow she and her sister played out in the rain, moving boulders and damming streams. They wore their plastic macs over their shorts and Wellington boots. When they were by the sea she enjoyed playing on the beach and the walks in the evening with her mother and the treats, sometimes a Crunchie or a Fry's five centre bar with delicate fondant cream inside in five different flavours. She tried to remember which order they were in. She and her sister had been allowed to choose which chocolate bar they would like, not have it decided for them as was usually the case. They were luxuries that at no other time could be afforded. While her father would read the paper and have a smoke, her mother would read to her daughters and they would listen and be sorry when she stopped because she was hoarse. They would play games at a table, converted out of the roof rack, four wing nuts securing the legs in position. She and her sister would have a new colouring book and a pack of crayons and would sit at the roof rack quietly. A cooking arrangement was cleverly devised so that her mother could continue with her culinary skills without complaining of kneeling down. "No peace for the wicked," she would say.

Only once did they holiday in England. It was the hot summer of '59 and they camped near Christchurch. The grass was yellow, dry and prickly. Her mother bought a second-hand bone china Minton breakfast cup and saucer in an antique shop for her husband. It was green with flowers and birds and looked Chinese. It cost £5. Her husband would have told her that she was bloody stupid, wasting her money. She didn't tell him. These were the only holidays that she remembered, no hotels, no guest houses, no holiday camps, no caravans, the reason being that it cost very little money. This was all her mother could afford. She used to say that they would have their own house if it wasn't for her father squandering his money on cigarettes, having a drink and putting petrol in the car. She felt ashamed of him. To her, these things were a waste of money, not necessary and likewise he thought that spending money on anything else was.

A long time ago, holidays abroad, like phones, belonged to rich and/or professional people who could afford the time and/or the money on the luxury. Her family fell into neither category. Her mother had a friend called Mrs. Jones. She fell into that category. She lived in the Old School House which used to be the village school for the first half of the century but in the early fifties the new school was opened, then the old school served as the church hall and Mrs. Jones's house. Mrs. Jones was the headmistress and cruised regularly during the long summer holidays. On returning from her holidays she would invite them to tea and show them, not her father, her slides on the projector set up in her sitting room. The heavy lined curtains were drawn to prevent the late August sunshine filtering in and spoiling the show. The projector hummed as the views were thrown up on a white rectangular screen, which operated like a roller blind on a tripod. They were filled with awe as they were transported across Europe to the Greek Islands, Venice, Athens and Rome. These were only places heard about in the Bible or Greek Mythology or in a game called Touring Europe, a sensible game given to her by her cousin, a teacher. Each player had a small racing car and a set of cards randomly dealt and the idea was that you had to plan your route to and from London and the first car home was the winner. Simple, really. The slide show was followed by tea served at the table in the dining room, when good manners were expected. Mrs. Jones had a gold tea trolley which she wheeled in from the kitchen, laden with thin, thin slices of brown bread and butter cut neatly in triangles overlapping each other, a jar of chocolate spread, (unheard of in her house) bought iced fancies in their own paper cases, slices of coffee and walnut cake and chocolate fingers. She had a liking for these tasty morsels and wondered why she didn't have these confections for tea at her house. Mrs. Jones brought back presents for her mother. She could remember a dark red Venetian glass vase and a glass paperweight, fish and reeds trapped between molten glass. It was the thing in those days to bring a memento back to friends and send postcards. The purpose of visiting new places seemed solely to traipse around the shops looking for interesting knick-knacks, a raffia napkin ring, a piece of local pottery, 'a present from Caernarfon' etched in white on a blue mug or a white handkerchief with a sprig of heather embroidered on the corner.

This was how it used to be. Now that she had grown up and aged, she had dispensed with a lot of things from those days. She had her own ideas and values. In her early teens she would not have imagined herself seeing the world. She imagined her life ahead much like her mother's, working, toiling and struggling, everything against her. Girls, especially girls like her didn't stand a chance. Not able to pass her eleven plus and go to the grammar school, she was written off. Mrs. Jones told her mother that in the exam she only wrote her name on the paper. In those days girls like her were not encouraged to sing and dance, to fulfil their dreams. For them, the route was already decided; leaving school at fifteen for a dull, dead-end job, working in a shop or a factory, giving up a proportion of your meagre wages for your keep then saving the rest, which wasn't much, until the right boy came along and if you were lucky, not finding yourself in the family way before the happy day. She did not want that life for herself, a life of drudgery, a penniless existence, never free from perpetual worry and anxiety. Even when she was young she lusted after ambition and dreamed of success and adventure, far away places, a life not like the one she had; nor did she not want to become like her mother.

In *la placa* she wrote her mother a postcard, just the usual things like the weather and the journey. She had promised to send a card each day and to ease the burden she had pre-typed some sticky labels with her grand address on. Ideally her mother would have something in the post every day. She knew in her heart it wouldn't be quite like that but that was the plan. For a start it would take a week for the first card to arrive and on some days she might receive two. She really knew that it would become too much like a chore to write every day. The grand address was where she lived now, a residential home with extensive grounds, her days spent looking out over the garden, watching the birds and the squirrels go about their daily routine, foraging and playing. In between looking out she focused on the television placed in the corner of the green room, its sudden brightness forever moving and the volume excessive. Unable to think straight she would have to find

31

the remote and reduce Flog It to a whisper. After a busy day it was the last thing she wanted to hear when calling in on her mother. The television seemed out of place in the gentle serenity, its wide flat screen, its hard plastic stand and a remote control which so often was mistaken as a glasses case and put in a handbag to be lost forever.

The room seated about twelve residents, the chairs arranged in twos and threes around the edge. They were high-backed and the fabric looked spongable, especially designed to resist any accidents. Small, square cushions, fat with foam, sat on most. Some residents had their favourite chair and were quite put out if someone else was in it. Her mother was one of them. She sat by the window and complained bitterly if Mrs Wood or Mrs Carr sat in her chair. She could be difficult and quite unreasonable at times, creating a fuss until one of the staff heard the commotion and came in to console her; like a spoilt child really. In spite of her at times, cantankerous ways, she remembered her mother fondly, frail and elderly now, struggling with old age, vulnerable as she had always been. A few years ago she had stopped looking after herself. She clearly couldn't be bothered and was increasingly relying on other people for support. Every Saturday, she would go and visit for a couple of hours, make her mother a cup of tea and sit with her or do some jobs which she could no longer manage, like changing the bed or doing the garden. She found this time extremely stressful and was thankful when she was back in her car driving home. She resented giving up her time, a quarter of her weekend spent without anything in return. She did it because she felt she ought to. She felt sorry for her, alone all week, not house bound, but not that able either, no longer participating in the community and being useful. Also, she couldn't bear the thought of letting the side down and her mother having to explain to her friends, why her daughter didn't visit. She knew that her mother would try to cover up and make excuses for her absence. She went, to avoid feeling racked with guilt. Her conscience would be eased and she would be free until the next Saturday when her tension and anger resumed once again.

She let herself in via the front door, the back being so barricaded against thieves and murderers, entering would have been impossible. The hall was narrow, with rugs protecting the carpet below. A heavy curtain prevented the door from opening fully and was a nuisance when carrying shopping as it would suddenly spring back unexpectedly. A gilt-edged mirror and a dark wooden barometer hung on the cream emulsioned walls. Besides heating the bungalow, the radiator was strung with fresh ironing, hankies and tea towels pressed into crisp, knife-edge folds. In one corner there was a triangular shaped cupboard, painted a lovat green to match the hall doors. This housed the electricity supply and bits and pieces which she didn't know what to do with, basically rubbish. On top of the cupboard stood a vase which had seen better days. Around it was a ribbon, the remnant of a bouquet from long ago and pending charity envelopes. As she had got older she had been persuaded by the adverts to give generously, and she had, feeling sorry for the stamp sized image portrayed and donating way beyond her means. In spite of the cheery hello, her mother would be unaware that she had even come in and would jump with surprise and say that she hadn't heard her come in. She sat in her usual winged chair by the table, wedged in position with cushions, her leg resting on a springy tubular stool draped with a travelling rug. She could tell her mood by the tightness of her jaw. She was often sullen, unspeaking, as though she had forgotten how to, just staring and fretting, her ill-fitting teeth moving around and constantly dabbing the edge of her mouth with a crumpled hankie. Her mother did not always reply and she would say, "Did you hear me?"

"Of course I heard you," she would answer, sharp and brusque, making her feel apologetic and sorry and stupid.

33

She hadn't heard and she would try and guess what the conversation was about. Out of sheer irritation her daughter would write things down and show her mother what she was talking about because she was sick of not being heard and understood. This infuriated her mother. Her mouth would tighten and she would look cross and disagreeable. She was easily annoyed, and even had something to say about the road sign which showed elderly people crossing. She did not see herself as being old and frail. She did have a hearing aid, bought years ago but it was too small and fiddly for her to manage. The sheer cost of it alarmed her and when her mother stayed with her daughter it was never seen again. Her sister's dogs, Molly and Elizabeth thought the smelly new chewy on the bedside table was great fun and proceeded to demolish it. Usually fond of dogs, her mother saw them in a new light and from then on gave them the cold shoulder. Investment in a second hearing aid proved just as frustrating. She knew what all her answers would be anyway and she felt sorry that her mother was not going to surprise her and say something to the contrary. In between their bursts of communication there were dreadful silences, at times so unbearable that she would suddenly stand up and announce that she was leaving and would see her next week. She would gather her things, kiss her mother goodbye and flee. Why did she feel so inadequate, so unable to speak to her, so lost for words. What did her mother think about for hours and hours and when asked she would just say, "Oh! Nothing."

Without success, she encouraged her mother to be active and take an interest in the world. Once, she bought her a cross stitch tapestry, a country garden, to occupy her fingers. A peeved look crossed her face. She had done the wrong thing. Her mother did not mince her words. Her daughter encouraged and cajoled and coaxed as kindly as possible and her mother relented. She disliked being told what to do and who could blame her? All her life she had been told what to do and when to do it and to be honest, she had had enough but at the same time her daughter only wanted the best for her. The little picture was not cross stitched with love, but in an angry temper. She lost her patience many times and practically threw it at her daughter on completion. Encouragingly, her daughter took it and would have liked to have put it straight in the bin, but instead praised her efforts and suggested a frame to show off the hard work. It disappeared under the seat of the car and was lost. Her mother never asked about it. When she could be bothered, she enjoyed reading, especially authors like Danielle Steel, glamorous and steamy in cities never seen. Even the covers of the books had a smart sophisticated look; strong colours with a gold embellishment, so opposite to her own life, often so drab and dull. Maybe in her silences, she reflected and wished, and knew that it was too late, too late to undo and change the past, her years slipping and her health deteriorating.

Her mother's life had been hard and thankless. The man she lived with was a tyrant; it was a word that her mother used frequently to describe him. How could she have married him? They were so opposite to each other. They had different values, different ideals, different aspirations. Even when she was young, a child, she remembered the verbal fights, constantly arguing, usually about money and the lack of it. Her mother did everything for him and gave him everything she had. She bent over backwards to ensure that his life was comfortable. He wanted for nothing. She had become trapped, caught up in a cycle and there was no way back, no escape from purgatory. She had to put up with him and endure the subservient existence that had become normality.

***

When she was thirty, she came to England as though emigrating from a native land She came partly because of the freezing cold of the east coast of Scotland and partly and more importantly to get away from her mother and start a new life. She found herself a very good job as a housekeeper at an expensive boarding school, she was independent and free at last until, like Eve, she was tempted and she paid the ultimate price. Today, society is much more liberal and tolerant. Unexpected babies and babies born out of wedlock are not called bastards or illegitimate, but they were then. She must have been filled with anguish, her escape plan had gone horribly wrong, there was no one to confide in and support her in her torment, no one to say you'll be all right, or console her or pity her. She felt wretched and totally devastated, the daily nausea draining her resources, her changing body, explaining the shape, explaining the shame. The new life she had so desired dissolving into another life, so unprepared for. Towards the end of her pregnancy she stayed in a nursing home for unmarried mothers. She, and others like her in the same agonizing boat, were stoned as they walked through the village, their new lives below their maternity smocks disgraced before they were born. The disgraced babies were placed for adoption. Wealthy childless couples would be updated on availability. They would look round the nursery and choose one as though they were ordering a piece of meat from the butcher. They could obviously afford all the modern comforts of the day. They would probably have a nanny too and a frilly nursery and a garden. Her mother could not give up her baby daughter. She sent for some of her belongings and a roomy canvas trunk, stamped with her initials was sent south in December 1950. She was not returning home.

She moved away with the baby's father to a small village where they were not known and set up home in a small terraced house and called themselves Mr and Mrs. Another baby was born two years later. The rented house was small. Two steps led straight off the pavement into the sitting room and in spite of the desperate need for space, she never remembered that room being used; it was kept for best in case visitors called, and had an unused smell, stale and earthy. They didn't make a habit of using the front door and preferred the back entrance and the path which joined all the houses. The rooms were small and the stairs led from the back room up to the smaller of the two rooms. The other bedroom was slightly larger; there was a double bed pushed against the wall. On it was a slippery green bedspread and eiderdown to match. She and her sister shared the back room, two really heavy sprung beds were bolted on top of each other to save space. There was a green carpet in the best room, but elsewhere there was lino. She remembered having a bath in front of the fire in the back room. The metal bath hung on a nail on the back door. Her parents never had a bath. A table fitted under the stairs and because they were small, she and her sister sat right under the stairs on a bench at mealtimes. The kitchen was basic and a geyser fixed to the wall heated the water. There was a toilet at the end of the yard. Even though she was only four she still remembered having to go in the middle of the night, turning the big key in the lock, seeing through the dark, feeling her way, disturbing no one. The toilet was basic, just a wooden board with a hole cut out. She remembered playing in the dirt at the back door with a girl called Mary, wearing an oatmeal coloured jumper with Muffin the Mule across the front. Not only did her mother use oatmeal to coat the fish, but also to describe the colour of her jumper. It fastened on the shoulder with three glass buttons. She remembered very little from that house, although whenever she sees sorrel it reminds her of roaming the wasteland behind the row of houses and collecting the dried rusty seeds in a jewellery box with her sister. Both parents worked in the next village, her father's hours slotting around her mother's so that there was always a parent at home. The landlord decided to sell and there was an opportunity to buy the property. Her mother was keen; she would have loved to have bettered herself and could see that buying her own home was a step in the right direction.

***

But that didn't happen. "We had the chance to buy our own house," her mother would say years later. However, they did move closer to their jobs to save the bike ride. Her mother settled into her routine, always up early, cleaning daily before going to work, coping, tired, with the endless pressure. As she and her sister grew so the tension between them was more obvious; their daddy was blatantly horrible to their mummy. They tended to side with their mummy. She was quite a different person with them. She read stories and poems to them. She and her sister would kneel down beside her lap and listen intently, not wanting her to stop. They went for long walks. She took her walking stick and would use it to point out wild flowers. In the late summer they gathered brambles to make jams and jellies. Determined, she would lean into the bush, unafraid of the thorns brushing her bare arms and the sudden plunging ditches along the hedgerows. She reached with her knotted walking stick to hook down the furthest briars heavy with berries, ripe and untouched by other pickers. Gently she would tease the berries from their core and deposit them safely in the basket. Once home, she weighed the fruit to assure herself that it had all been worthwhile. She had certainly worked hard enough for it. Then she would boil up the fruit in a jelly pan and use a saucer by the open window to test for setting. Sometimes, she made bramble jelly. She strained the juice through a knotted stocking and suspended it over her large mixing bowl, letting the dark purple juice drip all night. She would then continue in the morning, early, before anyone was up. The rough hard seeds were squeezed to get every last drop, then the congealed mass was discarded. The juice in the bowl was rich and black. Donated jars were washed and dried, the boiling jam or jelly ladled carefully and cleanly into them.

38

Once cold, a disc of waxed paper was placed on top of each jar and jam pot covers applied by wetting a circle of cellophane and stretching it over the neck of the jar then securing with a rubber band. Her hands would be stained, her bitten nails purple. Lemon juice was used to remove the worst. She would squeeze and twist a cut lemon around her blunted finger tips until the acid bleached and restored her skin.

She and her sister were not allowed to play with the other children in the avenue, only the neighbour's children on one side. There was no going into other people's houses. They had to entertain themselves in the house or the garden. Her mother felt that they were socially better than them, more refined, more cultured. They dressed differently. She and her sister wore kilts, not kilted skirts but real kilts made by McKewans of Perth and sent in the post in brown cardboard boxes, in their own tartan, the Ancient Baird. Now no one in the avenue could boast of that accolade. No, they were different all right. Her mother thought that most of the people in the avenue were bordering on gypsies or tinkers. Maybe some were; some families were Irish and that didn't help. Maybe she thought they were all Irish. The Scots and the Irish do not always see eye to eye. The girls played with a girl called Pin, named because she was so thin, like a pin. They played around the garages, between their houses. They had nothing to play with. The precious dolls were not allowed outside the gate, no, they played with rubbish that they found, or made up games. They did this for hours. She never went into Pin's house. Sometimes Pin had to have her tea in the shed. She was adopted and didn't sit at the table with her brother, who was not her real brother and his parents.

On a Saturday night Pin's dad worked at the 'Cali', a place famous for its ballroom dancing and the rising stars of the sixties. He worked as a barman. He had a car and worked at Vauxhall during the week, so they were considered prosperous. In the summer he would drop them all off, Pin, Pin's mum, Pin's not real brother, their dog called Sooty, her mother, her sister and her, at the bottom of the Downs and they would follow the white chalk paths all the way home and arrive back in the village just before dark. It was fun and exciting, running about, free, not being checked and reprimanded at every opportunity. At the end of the walk the two women continued to talk at the gate, her mother, transferring her weight from one leg to the other, nodding her head, saying "ah-ha" many times. The people in the avenue were good people, hard working and successful. When her mother moved to the bungalow where she lay bleeding all night, she used to visit the sick and frail in the very avenue where she once talked to no one. As the girls grew up so they visited friends after school. Their homes were not like their own. One family was very modern. They had a Bush television and instead of a Christmas tree, they had a branch that they suspended on the wall. They kept a rabbit in a hutch at the end of their garden and fed him dandelion leaves and they made models out of plaster in little rubber moulds, which when dry were pulled off carefully to reveal little characters which they then painted. She and her sister were not allowed any pets and they were not allowed to make a mess and they were not allowed anything that cost money. Her mother never liked coming home to her friends in the house and she made a scene, which made her and her friends awkward and embarrassed. Once she was allowed out to play, she was never in.

To her, her mother's friends were old or infirm or both and when visiting, she and her sister had to be quiet or go outside or sit still. These people had an assortment of biscuits which they kept stored in a biscuit barrel. She loved biscuits, they didn't have them in her house. They were only allowed two, no more. Any more would have been greedy. Her father did not accompany them on these visits, he didn't like her mother's friends. However, she did recall that he bought a car, the first of many bought on hire purchase, an agreement which permitted him the indulgence and pleasure of owning something. Apart from the clothes he stood up in, he didn't actually own anything. Until the car was paid for he didn't really own that either. Then, as soon as it was he would scour the garages for a new model and this was a constant bone of contention for her mother. She remembered several garages, one at the top of the hill and one on the Luton Road. When he turned left or right they used to chorus together, "Put your indicator down," until the orange indicator was restored to the slot in the side of the car. If she was on her own with her father she worried that if she didn't speak up he would curse and swear at her. She and her sister had to go with their father as they could not be left at home on their own, and they would sit in the car while their father stood and looked and talked small talk to the salesman. She remembered him deliberately sticking a G.B. sticker over a scratch on the boot of the car; he was no better than the salesman. He used to drive to Ashridge and picnic with these people that he couldn't stand, seeming to be generous and sociable and this could not have been further from the truth. Embarrassed, her mother tried to hide his blaspheming tongue and cover up for him, sometimes laughing it off, or changing the subject. While putting up with this behaviour at home, she didn't like other people to see him how he really was. She was utterly ashamed of him.

She always remembered her mother working, but the few shillings that she earned were not enough. Constant hardship and lack of money restricted her and prevented her having the things that during the fifties were becoming normal household goods; things like a vacuum cleaner or sheets. She would call her husband an old miser or a skinflint because he didn't give her any money at all. From time to time they took in lodgers, to make ends meet. She remembered Helen from Jedburgh in the Borders, her backcombed bouffant hair and her frothy net petticoats. She went jiving at the Cali and wore pointed stiletto heeled shoes. Helen was so modern and youthful, not at all like her mother. Her mother had taken to browsing through catalogues and ordering striped flannelette sheets, paying the smallest amount at the end of each month when it was pay day to a woman in the avenue who benefited from the commission. Her mother lost out either way, paying far more for the sheets or not having sheets.

1959 was a hot summer. It was the year when her mother, besides working all week, decided to take a weekend job as well. Her husband took her in the car about quarter to seven. They left their two young children in bed asleep. In the afternoon the girls went with him to collect their mummy. She remembered waiting for her on a Saturday afternoon listening to the sports report at five o'clock and the music dd dd ddddd ddddd dd and the announcer's dreary voice, Hamilton Academical 0 Heart of Midlothian 3, Partick Thistle 2 Queen of the South 1. In the same year she had her long hair which she had always worn up in a bun, cut off and permed short and frizzy. She never remembered her mother's hair as a bun and she never remembered seeing it loose, falling as it would have done over her shoulders. And the other thing was that she lost a lot of weight. She had always termed herself as stout and indeed she was tall and big boned, with thick legs and an ample bosom. Her Daddy called her ample bosom her paps and liked to unbutton her mummy's blouse and slip his hand between them. When her mother cuddled her, she was plunged into the soft heaving pillow, buried, drowning, suffocating, until the squeeze relaxed and she was allowed to surface and breath again. She kept her large shape strictly controlled in corsets and brassieres, each having at least a dozen hooks and eyes to contain the swimming flesh, giving a smooth firm silhouette. To attain this look there was much hoisting and tugging and pulling of the multi stitched cross-over, boned rubber architecture, feminised only by a rosebud motif in the centre. Stockings attached to the corset with suspenders, which had rubber buttons like those on a liberty bodice. There was nothing liberating about a liberty bodice. When the buttons perished with permanent use and old age she replaced them with ordinary buttons. She wore her heavy duty underwear well into her old age in spite of loving the feeling when she discarded it at bed-time for the freedom of her loose nightdress. Her clothes were the best she could afford. In the fifties she wore small prints on her big dresses and a white plastic belt around her thick waist. A neat hat perched over her bun and was kept in place with a hat pin. She always wore gloves to hide her worst habit. Her nails bitten to the quick in a worried frenzy, like a smoker desperate in a non-smoking building. Her nails now, glamorous and painted, freshly filed each week into perfect ovals, setting off her fine bony hands. Red was her favourite polish, not wishy-washy pearly pinks and apricots. Maybe she could at last be herself, bold and rebellious before it was too late, not unexpected. The mainstay of her wardrobe was the tweed skirt and blouse; she preferred tan and mustard, browns and beiges, to navy and black. She bought fabric and made her own clothes because it was cheaper. She never allowed herself the luxury of buying something off the peg until she could afford it. The thinner mother of the late fifties was on a constant diet to retain her desired weight. Always tired, from working seven days a week, grim faced and easily irritated. However, her sacrifices were worth it or so she thought. She could start affording carpets, a fridge and even a T.V.

Instead of feeling good, sitting in the midst of stunning scenery, having been well fed on a full English breakfast at seven a.m. cooked for her and her husband by Tom who, when he wasn't cooking breakfast, spent most of his day curled up like a cat opposite the T.V. in the corner and the temperature soaring, she didn't; she felt old. At first she put it down to the way she was dressed. She thought her loose calf length cargo trousers were ideal. They had a neat toggle

43

trim, which adjusted to the size of her waist, which was just as well as they had been discarded by her son and she had thought that they were too good to throw away or send to a charity shop. They were a suitable shade of green and she wore them with a selection of vests purchased from her local Tesco branch; three for five pounds. Although there was nothing wrong with how she looked, it wasn't her. To her she looked like other women in their middle years trying to be cool and young again. The close fitting vests accentuated her shape and in spite of being moderately lean and fit, to use a modern expression, she did not like drawing attention to herself. She didn't like people seeing her shape and tended to fold her arms or carry a bag close to her body to hide or disguise it. As the morning wore on and the heat intensified, so she became cross with her appearance, not that anyone could see her sitting in the reeds and longed to change into something light and cool. Impossible. Also, there were flies that sat and disturbed her thoughts, immune to the liberally-applied insect repellent. She also felt dissatisfied with herself for consuming for her, such a large breakfast with absolutely no way of burning up its energy. She felt sluggish and sedentary, just doing what so many old people do, just sitting, daydreaming, reading and sleeping, not speaking very much and only when necessary, when something like thirst or hunger became important.

Tranquil and wonderful though it was, she was restless. Her energy reserves were high. She wanted to break away, to escape the harsh sun and sweltering heat. The trouble was that she had too much time on her hands. She was used to an active day at work followed by making a meal and household chores in the evening, not leaving time to think. It was too quiet. She felt isolated and subdued. She and her husband didn't do chatting for the sake of it and the long unbroken silences became unbearable. She wanted to explode, such was the intensity of her emotions. Sometimes she spoke unnecessarily; she knew that as soon as she started to speak that it was a mistake, an obvious comment, no need to say anything at all. Blind speechless panic set in. If only she could swallow the words that she had just blurted out, but they had escaped to be mocked and laughed at. She remembered feeling like that when she was small – or not really small – more like when she was seven or nine, when her father would suddenly ask her the time out of the blue. She looked at the clock on the mantelpiece. What did it say? What did it say? Was it twenty past eight? Or was it twenty to four? The hands looked nowhere in particular, not on an exact number. She didn't know. What could she say? He knew that she didn't know. Inside she was writhing. She took a wild guess and it was wrong. That numb feeling spread through her, a gut wrenching feeling. Her father cursed under his breath. She truly was made to feel stupid. She felt sad and depressed. Why couldn't she just be honest, just be herself and say that she didn't know what the time was and why did she need to know anyway? If only there had been some fun attached to learning she might have been more successful at it. Most children had rubber rings when they were learning to swim or parents that held their children giving them confidence but not her. Two inflated leather footballs were tied tightly around her to keep her afloat. She remembered feeling absurd. Why couldn't she just be like the other children on the beach. Thank God children today do not have to endure such painful swimming aids. By the time she left junior school she still couldn't swim. She would lunge at the bar, flailing madly before she sank without trace. She didn't master swimming until her own children were competent swimmers. Now she has no fear. Reading diverted her thoughts, thoughts that plunged into the past. Disturbing and unsettling, unspeakable thoughts that chewed and gnawed at the depths of her soul. In her heart, she knew that this was the cause of her anguish and not a subject that could be comfortably broached, so she sat and read and kept her tormented thoughts to herself, spilling tears.

Her father was not tall, not as tall as her mother and apart from his stomach, he was not fat. His stomach protruded suddenly then went in again to his thin spindly legs. He stood upright, his broad shoulders firmly back, his regimental days had taught him how. Grooming was a performance, shaving every morning at the kitchen sink. He collected his toiletries together and put the kitchen towel on the draining board beside him, ready to dab and blot. He wore a white vest tucked into his trousers. He released the braces which held up his trousers so that they dangled like reins, down by his sides. He adjusted the round magnifying mirror. He ran some warm water in the washing up bowl and rubbed his dampened shaving brush into the bar of Sunlight soap, lathering thick white foam and liberally applying it to his face and neck. Then he took his razor and dipped it into the warm water. He cut into the foam cleanly and deliberately. He rinsed off the surplus lather from the razor and cut again and again until his face was free of foam and his reflection stared back, pink and smooth. With both hands, he splashed his face, water running down and dripping off his elbows onto the floor. He picked up the towel and patted his face dry and he felt it with the palm of his hand, looking at himself as he did so. He was so vain. He loved himself so much, he would prune and preen, trimming his nasal hair and his moustache, filing his nails, checking his feet. She remembered once, that he had a wart on the side of his nose and he tied a piece of thread around it, starving it of blood until it looked like a currant and dropped off. What little hair he had was cut weekly by a man who charged very little. Very rarely did he go out without a bonnet on, (sounding like punnet but spelt with a b). In other words a flat cap or sometimes a trilby to cover his receding hairline. He wore specs with thick tortoiseshell frames and when it was sunny, he made a pair of tinted glasses without the arms, which hooked on. His shoes were made of leather; good strong shoes made to last, brogues with laces, cleaned every morning by his wife on her hands and knees.

Her mother cleaned all the shoes every morning before she went to work. It was one of the routine jobs, along with cleaning the grate and dusting. She lined them all up and cleaned them vigorously, applying the polish first out of a little round tin with a picture of a kiwi on it, then letting it dry off, then brushing furiously until they gleamed, and woe betide you if you had dog shit on your shoe. Her mother never said that word, but her father said it all the time. Around the house her father was lazy; he expected everything to be done for him. "He doesn't think of anyone but himself," she would grimace and shake her fist behind his back. Once the ablutions had been completed he would have a cigarette and read the Daily Telegraph from cover to cover. He would scrutinize the births, marriages and deaths columns with care, in case he missed a name that he recognized from the past. On Sundays he would enjoy the News of the World, with its saucy innuendo and glamorous girls. He filled in the Pools coupon and checked the football results. Needless to say, her mother did not approve. She maybe thought that it was a substitute for her not being there on a Sunday morning doing her duty and fulfilling his needs. The newspapers were delivered by Percy Smith or rather Shaky Smith, as he was known, because he was so shaky. She did not approve either, of his friends, who were Irish, over here to build the M1. Nothing short of gypsies her mother would say, over here to make a new life for themselves, living in squalor, children born every year into homes with mud floors instead of lino. He would go drinking with these pals and stay out until the early hours. These men were rough and earthy, their fast talking foreign language in unintelligible accents. If they talked to her she just smiled meekly so as not to seem rude. Often her father came home drunk, unable to stand up. Looking back, how he could have driven the car was beyond her. She recalled her mother helping him up the stairs and the two of them falling as they reached their bedroom door, him heavy and slurred, awkward and clumsy to support, her mother cursing and crying. Her mother objected to his habits, supping tea out of a saucer and dipping bread and butter in granulated sugar. His table manners, so important to her, were appalling.

They were rarely out as a family and unless the weather was really warm and sunny he wore a wool gabardine trench coat. It was big and roomy, ideal for pocketing things that were not his, and he did. She saw him once when she was ten, pick up a book and slide it underneath the front of his coat and into the big deep poacher's pocket inside. She stared at him in disbelief. Of course her daddy did not look like a regular criminal. He was smartly dressed in good clothes, shirt and tie, shiny shoes. Even Nora Batty didn't trust a man with shiny shoes. These days CCTV would be on his case straight away and he would not get away with it. His wife knew that he stole because he spent all his money on drink, cigarettes and his car, so coming home with anything else must have been stolen. What need did he have for a book or a leg of lamb? It was a habit that his wife found distressing. She simply dreaded the thought of a police car drawing up outside the house and having to explain and people in the avenue gossiping. She could not have coped with the shame.

Mealtimes were formal and agonising. The radio which sat on the sideboard was on and you were expected to listen. Meals were served at the large oak table, which extended fully to an oval. They usually sat at the biggest half and like the shoes, it was highly polished. The four places were laid with cork mats covered with melamine to protect the table, in a traditional flowery Goya style. Two slightly larger mats were laid for the vegetable dishes. The cutlery was also traditional, in sterling silver, and needed cleaning with Duraglit every now and then to remove the tarnish. She always remembered cleaning the cutlery on Christmas Eve; six table forks, six dessert forks, six dessert spoons and several serving spoons. No knives, she couldn't remember the knives. Yes she could; they had bone handles and didn't need cleaning, couldn't have been sterling silver. She also had to clean the four initialled napkin rings which were silver. The table looked lovely and Christmassy, and no expense was spared. Christmas was a lavish affair and like the summer holidays was scrimped and saved for all year. The girls were treated alike and had identical presents so that they could not argue. Their dolls had cots, hand made by their father and painted blue. They were sturdy and used up surplus timber from the shed. The lace edged sheets and bed linen were hemmed well into the early hours of Christmas Day by their mother, dolls fully kitted out in new dresses made out of old. Of course it didn't last. Once hogmanay was over the rot set in again and the nice friendly family atmosphere was put away with the decorations and, "We'll have to tighten our belts". So the nice blip ended for another year and the tarnish returned. The initials on the cutlery handles always intrigued her. Must have come by them in an auction or a second-hand shop. She still had them now, in her kitchen drawer, wrapped in an orange coloured Reveal Records bag. She knew now, where they had come from.

She and her sister would sit at the table silently, without any fuss. The one thing that her mother did outstandingly well was to improvise food for her family. It seemed to come out of thin air, as there never seemed to be anything in the house to actually eat. The ridicule would come thick and fast.

"Christ almighty woman. There's no bloody salt on the table."

"Why didn't you tell me it was bloody hot?"

"Jesus Christ woman, there's no bloody sugar in the tea," lifting his hand to strike her. He didn't.

"I'm not eating that bloody shit," pushing his plate away, the ultimate insult.

At the back of the cupboard under the sink was the Thermos flask, still stained brown from Typhoo tea drunk long ago. It was made of tin and had greaseproof paper wrapped round the cork stopper because it always leaked. It was used on afternoons out when they would drive just a few miles and park the car. The travelling rug would be laid on the grass beside the car so that her parents had something to lean against while they drank their tea. Sometimes her parents would fall asleep in the car, watching the view. She and her sister would look for treasure and collect wild flowers. Once, when they were going on holiday the flask and the bacon sandwiches, such a luxury, were left on the draining board, forgotten.

"Jesus Christ Almighty. You silly bloody woman."

Of course it was her mother's fault. Everything was.

She was so hurt and vexed by his insults but never tired of wanting to please, attentive at any opportunity, arranging the teaspoon on the right side of the saucer, or the handles of the serving spoons positioned for him to use first. Taking out the bones of his fish, fetching his shoes and putting them by the back door. He wanted for nothing. She was there to please, like a servant at his beck and call. No please or thank you, no love. Besides his insulting behaviour and caustic expletives he would make long and extended belches and 'gwarting' noises and not say excuse me or pardon me or I'm sorry. He would fart and enjoy the fact that she was breathing in his polluted air. He was never sorry and never said that he was sorry. He showed no remorse. He felt that it was his divine right to humiliate her mummy like that.

He was an army man, a disciplinarian. "A man's man, an intelligent man." her mother would say as though she wasn't capable of having an intelligent conversation with him. "His bark is worse than his bite." Why did she always stick up for him? Why did she marry him? Could she not see that he was a bully and she was the victim. He was a loser. The relentless abuse left its mark, nerves frayed and never repaired, her deep animosity towards him drained her of all emotion. At the end of her tether she would let rip, "You're contemptible John." Or, "You're insufferable John," said with venomous hatred.

She put on a brave face. No-one knew about her intolerable existence on the other side of the front door. Her house reflected her life; on the surface it was clean and polished, but open a cupboard or a drawer, or look under a cushion or behind the settee, it was all there, the clutter, the flotsam, accumulated and drifting relentlessly, clogging up and stifling her. Even when she was small she remembered the glory hole by the back door. The cupboard extended under the stairs. It was big. These days it would be transformed into a flat pack office and a computer installed but then it was absolutely full of dirty washing. There had been a laundry basket once, but it lay buried underneath the mountain of smelly clothes and stale flannelette sheets. She had no means of washing anything other than using her bare hands. There was a mangle in the garden. No wonder the washing sat, waiting to be done. The drawers were stuffed full, they were roughly made and difficult to open and even more difficult to shut. All the drawers were in the same state of chaos, whether it was the sewing machine drawers upstairs or the kitchen drawers. You couldn't put your hand on anything without a major upheaval. Cupboards were the same. Nothing had any logic, nothing had a specific place, dishes and pans were just launched in, out of sight and the door shut.

Even important documents were put randomly behind the clock or in the book case or under a cushion and lost forever. When she went to visit her mother she would sometimes have a tidy, just plump up the cushions and sort the magazine rack. There were endless envelopes, some with things in, others empty, countless Christmas cards and birthday cards, opened and read then replaced in the envelope and hidden under cushions along with inserts from newspapers, parish magazines and pairs of tights which she had shed in the privacy of her own room but then stuffed out of sight so that no one would see.

It was her mother's desire to continue to work as long as she could and, although her weekend job stopped on retiring age at sixty, she continued her full time job until she was sixty five. By then, of course, her father was eighty. She would escape to her daughters' homes and leave him to fend for himself.

***

Quite recently, when her mother was eighty-seven and she was fifty-four, her mother leaned forward in her chair and grasped her hand and squeezed it tight and said to her, "I love you Connie." She was surprised and taken aback. She allowed her hand to stay wrapped in hers, gripped and held. This surely was the first time that she had ever said it. She felt awkward, she didn't know how to reply. "I know you do," she finally said, not truly convinced. Only her husband had told her that he loved her and that was a long time ago. Maybe she had to say before it was too late. She might forget or she might die that night and her daughter, precious enough fifty-four years ago not to be taken away for adoption, would never know. Why did she leave it so long? Once she had said it, it was not so difficult to say the next time and the time after that and the time after that. When she said it she smiled with pride and absolute joy, deep heartfelt joy that surfaced through her troubled elderly mind. She seemed immersed in difficulty. She longed to know what lay below the surface and sometimes said, "What are you thinking about?"

Her mother would reply, "Oh, nothing," or, "Oh, this and that." She would always close the curtain on her thoughts. She must remember to tell her own children that she loved them, as indeed she did. She worried before her first son was born that she wouldn't be able to love her husband and her baby equally or more than or less than, but when her son was born and the subsequent babies that followed were born, it was pure unadulterated love, a delirious, extravagant love, which for her, had to be the most exquisite emotion, the most ultimate feeling of all time. The love for her husband continued as before. This delirious feeling might have passed her by.

When her mother started working at the weekend she was eight, her sister was six, her mother was forty-two and her father was fifty-seven. It was the start of the abuse that lasted three years. Of course she didn't know it was abuse then. She had never heard of the word. She shared a bedroom with her sister. The space saving bunk beds of the previous house were collapsed into two single beds, one each side of the room against the walls, allowing space between to play. Each bed had the candy striped sheets, paid for in instalments, and pink taffeta quilts. Their teddies, Bruin and Koala, sat in the corners by their pillows. Like bookends, they knelt at their beds and prayed every night. She didn't see what her sister did, but she pressed her hands together and closed her eyes and murmured

"This night before I go to sleep

I pray thee Lord my soul to keep,

And if I die before I wake

I pray thee Lord my soul to take.

God bless mummy and daddy,

Watch over me the whole night through

And always keep me close to you. Amen."

The room had not always been laid out in that position because she could recall when she had been very poorly with both whooping cough and mumps together, that her bed was behind the door, not facing the door. Everyone had been really nice to her when she had been ill. She felt special and cared for and even given her own box of chocolates. Besides earning more money, going out to work suited her mother. It meant that she no longer had to endure the physical and mental demands that her husband imposed on her.

***

Just because her mother wasn't there didn't mean that snuggling down in her parents' bed did not continue. He wasted no time. At the first opportunity her father stood there. Well are you coming, he would say, leaning over her, still in the clothes he had taken her to work in. Dutifully she left the safety of her cosy bed and quietly padded out of her room, the lino cold on her bare feet. Her parents' room overlooked the avenue at the front of the house. The curtains were closed and the grey light oppressive. Once used to it you could make out the shapes in the room. There was a big double wardrobe on her daddy's side of the bed and there was a recess in the corner which was curtained and where he hung his clothes, and years later where she found a pile of magazines of naked women flouncing and pouting. On her mummy's side of the bed there was a treadle sewing machine, which doubled up as a bedside table. On it was a lamp with a nicotine coloured parchment shade and a brown woven twisted flex. Opposite the window there was a small fireplace made of beige mottled tiles. It was never used but it was normal in those days to have fireplaces in most rooms because there was no central heating. At the end of the bed there was a dressing table in the same bulky style as the wardrobe, leaving only a small space to walk round to her mummy's side.

She climbed into the bed and lay down. There was still a deep warmth from where her mummy had lain. Her daddy changed back into his pyjamas and lay down beside her. This was not unusual when her mummy was there, but she wasn't and she had no idea of what was about to happen. Innocent, naïve, stupid, gormless. She was often called gormless and she hated it. Couldn't even tell the time, didn't even know that what he was doing to her was not all right, not normal. "We won't tell mammy now will we? It will be our special secret." The warm sticky fluid spewed out of him, violently, then dribbling until it lay in a pool. She didn't know what it was but the feeling obviously gave her daddy a thrilling sensation because his face would lose its shape and he would moan with pleasure and he would be nice when the episode had passed. He would even be nice to her mummy, when he collected her from work at five o' clock.

***

She did not know what boys looked like. It never occurred to her to think about boys other than just boys. Her daddy liked and encouraged her to touch his body, the part that lay amongst greying hair, the part that managed to change itself and go stiff and hard. "Play with me," he would say and she did, not knowing. Sometimes she stood beside the bed and took this part of his body in her mouth. She didn't like it. She didn't like the suffocating smell and the acrid taste of the shrivelled wrinkly skin. Her eyes were open, she could see his big hard stomach, then he started to move his bottom off the bed, rapidly and repeatedly, grinding and pushing, filling her mouth, until he was sick. That is what he called it. "Make me sick Connie. Oh! oh! go on, make me sick," He would whimper and gasp. He would lift up her nightdress and touch the innocent fleshy folds between her legs, prodding and pushing with his fat blunt

55

manicured fingers then he would get on top of her, forcing and thrusting. She could barely breath. He would be reduced to a pulp, reaching his oblivion, spewing out his sickness. Silently, she would slip out of his room and retreat to the safety of her own bed. "Don't let anyone interfere with you down there," he would threaten. He thought nothing of sliding his hand under her skirt and fingering inside her pants when she was washing up dishes at the sink. Once she felt her body responding, something deep inside her had been aroused. Silently she was losing control, her internal muscles contracting, her body deciding what to do, like an animal. The pulsating confusion inside her made her feel frightened and disgusted with herself, ashamed, yet strangely she liked the odd sensation. Nerves were made to tingle and dance. His authoritarian, will-do-as-I-say manner, was enough to make her obedient and conform. The threat was always there. He might have hit her. He often threatened to hit with the back of his hand, as he did with her mummy, muttering curses, just not quite having contact.

***

Maureen and Maud were twins and lived at the other end of the avenue. They were the daughters of the woman who had sold her mother the sheets. The three of them were walking home from school. The path was rough in places and sometimes they had to walk in single file. They dawdled and jostled along. Their class had been swimming and a coach had transported them to the local pool, a concrete lido painted blue set into the side of the Downs. Even though she couldn't swim, she enjoyed trying and it was a change from lessons. She remembered it being ice cold and needing such courage to wade into. It was so cold, in fact, that some children, including her, turned blue and their teeth would not stop chattering. Her mother always gave her some shortbread to control the clockwork teeth. She plied her new friends with shortbread; the bait. They were not her real friends but she thought that by sharing her shortbread and confiding her darkest secret with them that they would be interested in her and realise that there was more to the queer girl who wore a kilt. Surprisingly they did not seem bothered. What, to her, was the most awful ordeal, was insignificant to them and they went on to explain how their older brother could ejaculate (not that she knew that word at the time) and the sperm (or that word) would hit the ceiling. Now that was much more impressive. Confused and ashamed, she said goodbye and turned right. They were not her friends. Years later she wondered if Maureen and Maud ever thought of that afternoon. Maybe they thought she was lying.

So innocent and gullible was she that she didn't understand that she should tell someone anyway, and after all, her Daddy had said that it was their special secret.

She was eleven, her sister was nine, her mother was forty five and her father was sixty. Thankfully, with the onset of puberty, the physical abuse ceased and only once was she caught out. It was a bitterly cold snowy day when the school heating failed and everyone was sent home. She arrived home before lunchtime and sat by the fire to warm up. She sat on her daddy's knee and within moments his warm hand slipped underneath her school blouse and into her bra, cupping his fat manicured fingers around her breast, groping and searching for her nipple. She pulled away.

Off her guard one day she was taking photos with her friend with her new instamatic. It was the weekend and her mother was at work. It was her father's turn to be in the picture. Her friend reminded her of the girl on the front of her mother's South Pacific L.P. She had an oriental look, dark glossy hair, a tawny complexion and perfect features. Her friend stood beside him in the back garden in her shorts and blouse and 'V' necked cardigan. Her white ankle socks made her smooth bare legs look even browner. She would have loved to have white ankle socks like hers, she always had to have light blue or lemon. Her mother couldn't cope with white and one pair had to last all week. She peered through the lens. His arm was around her friend's slight frame, his hand clamped over her breast. Her friend looked awkward and uncomfortable. She couldn't believe what she had seen. She was so embarrassed and so ashamed of her father. She tried to pretend that she hadn't seen and turned a blind eye. Not surprisingly, the friendship ended.

She learned to avoid being at home alone with him. She learned to avoid contact nearly altogether, whether it was eye contact, speaking, anything, but out of the depths, another problem faced her. Her mother, who knew nothing of her wretchedness, encouraged her to be nice to her father. He deserved to be treated with respect, she said. "He is your father after all." She managed it only by not showing any emotion whatsoever to other people and especially for her mother's benefit. No one would have known that there wasn't perfect harmony between them. The perfect daughter. She felt nothing but contempt for her father. She loathed and despised him. She tolerated him purely to avoid a scene and to spare her mother a humiliating embarrassment. It was so hard letting other people think that he was the best thing since sliced bread. She was living a lie. As she got older she found it harder to believe that her mother could not have been aware. She must have known or suspected or got a feeling that something was not right. If she did suspect anything she never said. She let it go, to keep the peace.

***

Sometimes she thought about killing herself, because that would have solved everything, or running away.

Who would have cared, God knows? Both she and her sister were always being threatened with being put in a

58

home. She actually thought that a home might be have been preferable. It might have been fun with all the other children. Why did nobody recognize the signs? Why did no one follow up her lack of achievement? Why did she only write her name on the eleven plus paper? Who could she have told? Who could she have confided in? Who could she have trusted? There was no one, no one that would believe her, instead of her father. He was in the Masons, a secretive cult that gave him, or so he thought, power and clout. He wore a gold ring on his little finger, the centre of which rotated. On one side was a smooth oval of gold, on the other, a deep blue with a gold insignia. Even Maureen and Maud were contemptuous. Her mother would have just dismissed the whole thing as ridiculous and how could she imagine such a thing and call her a wicked girl and send her to wash her mouth out. No, there was no one, not even her own mother.

She remembered playing dominoes. She would be paired with her father.

"You can handle your father." Her mother would say, knowing full well that she would be spared the verbal abuse when she placed the five three or God forbid, the double six, even though she had no option. Maybe her mother thought that her daughter shared the same special relationship with her father that she had done with her own father.

When she could hang on no longer, she told her husband. She was in her thirties and her children were small, tucked up in beds and cots. For her, the decision to tell was heartbreaking and although never far from her thoughts, it was prompted unexpectedly from a situation that she had not before considered. Her sister's children were visiting their grandparents the following weekend and staying the night. Alarm bells. In a flash, she pictured the Sunday morning, the children up early and pestering their Grandma and her getting impatient and sending them

59

through to their Gradad for a cuddle. No, that could not be allowed to repeat itself. She had to reveal her hidden secret. She was distraught at the thought of the outcome. She sat quietly by the open fire. "I've got something to tell you," she said and sparing the graphic detail, she blurted out her torment through floods of tears. It was all over in a matter of minutes and the immediate relief was immense. At long last, after nearly twenty years with her husband, the deceit was exposed. He reacted as she knew he would. "Don't expect me to go there again," and true to his word, he didn't.

Her father took to his bed, her mother encouraged him and was pleased that she no longer had to look at his sour miserable face all the time. She continued with her weekly visits and her mother expected her to pop (as though it was nothing) through to his bedroom and say hello, and to please her she did, knowing that he would only have given her mother grief had she not done so. However, that meant being on her own with him. She had absolutely nothing to say; for her the passing of time had made no difference. Once again she stood beside the bed and was nice. She felt powerful. He lay there, his pink face slack and old, his head propped on flowery pillows, his hair white, pyjamas buttoned right up to his loose, hanging throat. A matching flowery duvet covered his shrinking, shrivelling bones. His glasses were on the cupboard beside the bed, his piggy eyes staring. She stared back in defiance, knowing that his sight was failing and that he probably only saw her as a blur. She wanted to scream and be as far away as possible. She had to find excuses why her husband no longer went to see them. Eventually, she decided to tell her mother. Increasingly, there were stories in the papers and on the television of people who had been abused and finally had the courage to speak. She felt that spilling the beans would help her mother understand why she was like she was, but it did nothing; it was just a story, like the ones in the papers. But she was in denial. She refused to acknowledge that her husband had done such damage to her daughter. Why, she was fit and healthy, she had a good husband, children, a home of her own, what more did she want? She supposed that it was good compared with her life but the fact that her mother failed to see or refused to see that what her husband had done to her daughter all those years ago, was unforgivable. She could see that her mother felt uncomfortable and spared her the sordid detail. She was quiet and subdued. She didn't really say anything that made her daughter feel better. She didn't even get off her chair and put her arms round her or even say she was sorry. Looking back, was it worth telling her? Maybe for her mother it was the final nail in the coffin. Surely life was not worth living.

Receiving this information was not so incredible. Her mother had something much more pressing to share with her daughter. In 1980 when he was seventy eight and she was sixty two they got married, not because they loved each other but because her mother did not want her daughters not to find a marriage certificate. She and her sister, both well into their middle years, could not have cared about a certificate. They cared much more about their mother's well-being and in fact, probably would have thought more of her had she not married, not, 'done the right thing.' The confession came about because her father's decree nisi had finally come through after sixty years of marriage. His first wife, probably past caring, had finally relinquished her hold. Her mother was three when he married in nineteen twenty just after his eighteenth birthday. Her mother didn't say any more. In 1951 when her mother and father had called themselves Mr and Mrs it would have been seen as a crime. For thirty years, her new life, which she had planned, had been a complete sham, her risky relationship waiting to be discovered, both daughters born illegitimately, and the trail of deception was more than she could bear. Had she been found out, she would not have been able to endure the consequences. He was responsible for the ruined lives and lack of trust. "His day of reckoning will come," she prophesied. This surprising revelation didn't mean that it was all right, it didn't make how she felt any easier, it just compounded her intense dislike for her father. If only her mother had not married him. If only she had reached out and confided in her daughters. They were there for her and she hadn't seen.

She sat with her mother in the small waiting room at the end of the ward. Her mother sat motionless in her navy coat, buttoned tightly. Like a claw, one knarled hand gripped her walking stick like a vice. Through the thin translucent skin she could see the bubbling blue veins and the whiteness of her knuckles. Her other hand clutched her handbag and her maroon velour gloves. As always, she wore a hat. The room was bleak. The drabness of the chairs scattered around, blended with the carpet and the walls and the gloomy December day. Her mother just stared blindly at the carpet without seeing it. The room overlooked a busy main road. Through the stark winter beeches she could see the cars and lorries turning left and right and going straight on, miming silently beyond the double glazing. She was restless and longed to escape the unfamiliar sterile vacuum, to breath the polluted air, to smell the exhaust fumes, to hear the frenzied revving of the cars and screeching brakes, to be living. They had barely spoken all the way to the hospital. There was nothing to say. A fresh-faced nurse hovered discretely and said that her father was ready. Her mother looked drawn. She helped her mother to her feet and slowly followed the nurse back along the ward, past the fragile patients leaning on their plumped up pillows, their eyes shut. They stopped at a bay with its curtains closed. The nurse walked briskly and was there before them. She held the curtains back while they filed in and stood beside the bed. His pithy life had finally come to an end. He lay there. He was bone white, the sheet was folded down and a flower had been placed on the pillow by his face. Did someone feel sorry for him? Did they think that he had been neglected? No flowers! No visitors! She looked at her mother and touched her arm. There were no tears, just a tired, worn out expression. She knew that Connie felt indifferent. She knew that she would get no sympathy from her daughter. Of course, she felt sorry for her. She was bewildered and confused by the train of events. Her daughter provided her with practical support and dealt with the funeral arrangements.

He was ninety eight when he died. No justice. There was a service in his memory, held in the local church on a cold Friday morning in December. People went to support her mother. Since her marriage, she had become involved with the church, attending regularly and praying for forgiveness. She was sure that her mother had been forgiven, her mother was not to blame, just as she was not to blame. They were both victims, caught up and entangled in a web of deceit. She had no emotion at the service. She didn't feel that it was right that such a blaspheming hypocrite should lie in his coffin in front of the altar. He was not a Christian. Afterwards she served endless cups of tea and coffee and provided seasonal Tesco's mince pies; the ultimate insult. Who cared anyway? The time after the funeral was intensely painful. Her mother never said how she felt, she was understandably confused and disinterested. Christmas followed and she invited her to stay. The atmosphere in the house was anything but joyous. Unable to cope with her irrational behaviour, she took her mother back home the day after Boxing Day. When the funeral director phoned, five years after his death she politely told him what he could do with her father's ashes.

Her mother was a prude and didn't tell her about the 'facts of life'. She felt very uncomfortable at the very mention of the subject. She found it distasteful and it was to be avoided at all costs. Even the leggy Pan's People on Top of the Pops were too much for her. The other day when Samantha Fox was being interviewed by Richard and Judy, she was perfectly charming, then the camera took a shot of her, erotic and barely dressed, lusting from the front of a glossy magazine. Uncomfortable and embarrassed her mother turned away. Even she had to admit that it was not suitable viewing for children coming home from school and the narrow-minded eighty somethings sitting in the green room. Her mother had let her down. After all it was the most important thing on earth. She knew nothing about her own body. She couldn't even name the parts, the parts that were becoming more noticeable and more sensual. She did nothing to warn her daughter of the impending monthly cycle and the implications, which she obviously knew all too well, if the monthly cycle ceased. She didn't even know where babies came from. In fact, she thought that oral contraception was taking the boy's thingy in her mouth. Understandable; oral, thus avoiding the risk; makes sense. Her mother had let her down big time, leaving her feeling ill-informed and totally unprepared, ignorant, a disaster really. Not even school provided the educational approach. She learnt as she went along.

***

Sometimes she felt like her mother. Indeed there was certainly a resemblance; the stoop, the rounded back and the twisted spine. Had her father slotted his army cane behind his wife's shoulders as he had her, trying to improve her posture and because of her structure, always looking at the ground, eyes averted, avoiding other people' glare? Her mother still looked at the ground, and if she saw something good like a five pence piece she would hone in on it, moving it with her stick or dislodging it with the sole of her shoe to make sure it was the real thing and not a piece of rubbish. Then she would bend forward and pick it up, pleased, and put it in her pocket. Even when her daughter took her out for a walk in her wheelchair, her eyes would scan the path for coins and treasure. From her vantage point she would point, "What's that?" and expect her daughter to investigate for her and report back. When she introduced her daughter to a new resident, "I know who you are," they would say, even before the hellos and pleasantries were exchanged. Was it that worryingly obvious? She felt like her mother when she wiped the table; big sweeping 's' shapes with a wrung-out dishcloth, then scooping the debris cleanly off the edge of the table into the palm of her left hand, and when she made cakes, beating the mixture violently with a large wooden spoon, the slapping sound on the sides of the bowl, her upper arms loose and flabby; not that hers were but that was the image that crossed her mind, imagining her arms flapping and slapping like the mixture in the bowl. She hoped that the children watching her demonstrate the creaming method didn't think about her arms like that. She knew that they might because she did at their age but unlike them, she would never had said.

Like her mother, she liked to please and rarely disappointed; meals prepared, the grass cut, the letter posted. Sometimes she felt pressured into doing things that she didn't want to do and she would do them to keep the peace just like her mother had done and that made her feel angry and resentful. She would feel annoyed with herself for not standing up to other people's demands. She did, however, enjoy the appreciation and the acknowledgement that her mother did not. She felt like her mother when she held her fork and put food in her mouth and when she bit into a slice of toast. She, like her mother, was the driving force, not contented to sit back and vegetate but forever improving, planning and striving for change. Her mother loved money. She loved money more than anything, She loved the power and the freedom that it gave her. She allowed herself to indulge and enjoy in giving and spending and when she had done that she started saving, saving passionately, lovingly counting and accumulating her money in envelopes and hidden under the cushions or in the airing cupboard. She had no money, just her pension and she went without in order to fuel her desire to save, forever striving.

She too, enjoyed her money and although most went on necessities, some went on treats like holidays or a fluffy jumper or a meal out. She recalled, however, falling into the same trap. She was probably fourteen and started keeping her dinner money, her only source of income. Starving herself, but no one noticed and no one cared. No one noticed children in those days. She was like her mother when something went wrong. She remembered lifting the heavy oval dish out of the oven and placing it on the wooden chopping board. She hadn't placed it quite far enough on the board and it slipped off, almost in slow motion onto the kitchen floor. She sobbed on her hands and knees, the duck breasts scattered around her, the orange sauce wasted, the dish broken. She was so vexed. Her mother would have said, "Ye gods and small fishes," and done exactly the same, gathered up the duck put it in a clean dish checking for shards of pottery and made a new pan of sauce and returned it to the oven to finish off. No one would be any the wiser. Although she was usually placid, very occasionally she would let rip and fly off the handle. She would come home from work to find that her selfish teenage children had left the kitchen in a complete mess. The work surfaces, the table, the draining board and the hob were completely covered in dirty dishes, congealed pans, toast crumbs and jammy knives. She was so angry that her first reaction was to sweep everything crashing to the floor. Installing a dishwasher sorted the problem. Her mother too, expected to find her kitchen as she had left it. She didn't like the lingering smells of eating a meal in the sitting room but occasionally she relented and took her husband his dinner on a tray so that he could watch the match on the television. She knew that she was being like her mother. She felt like her, checking the tray and ensuring that his every need was on it, the right amount of food cleanly placed, the cutlery and the condiments to accompany the meal, oh and the napkin in its silver ring. She remembered her children years ago, cutting out a picture of an old man wearing a moulded plastic bib with its own curled up tray designed to catch the drips of gravy or custard. They put the picture in his place at the table and waited for his comment. "I'm not like that yet," he would laugh. But now, when she sees a drip of gravy on his shirt or worse still, on a cushion, she smiles to herself and pictures the plastic bib, not such a bad idea, as long as it could go in the dishwasher. She didn't like the idea of being folded up on a soft seat and ate her dinner as usual, sitting upright or nearly upright in the kitchen.

She stood up all day and most of the evening. Her feet took a pounding. She was constantly filing and rubbing and smoothing then applying creams and lotions. Spending, she reckoned, more on her feet that her face. Her mother too stood all day, no such luxury for her, she lay a piece of newspaper on the floor then she sliced into her feet with a razor blade, holding it between her thumb and forefinger, concentrating, her mouth slightly open, saliva building in the corners, removing thin slivers of hard yellowing skin until her feet were smooth. She had inherited her varicose veins from her mother, and like her mother had had the unsightly bunches of grapes stripped out. For her, the procedure had taken twelve hours but back in the seventies her mother had been admitted to hospital for a week. She remembered seeing her when she had not long returned from theatre, still drowsy from the anaesthetic. She had been so upset at the sight of her lying there, looking dead and strange. She felt like her mother when she put on the vicious tights, worn afterwards to encourage the blood to flow normally again and although her mother would have worn stockings, it was the same way that she put them on, gathering up each leg right to the toe, slipping it over her foot, gently pulling until the fully fashioned heal slipped into place, snug and firm then gripping and pulling gently but firmly until the fabric gripped like a rubber band around her legs. She didn't like the friction of two fabrics rubbing against each other and wore loose linen trousers to hide them. To her, unless they were black, the thick denier tights looked old fashioned and frumpy.

When it came to preparing and serving food, her mother was renowned, it had to be just right. She did not like messy food and she didn't think much of the celebrity chefs on television. She would watch in horror as the food they prepared was messed about with. For perfect mashed potato one chef used four pans and containers. "Utter rubbish," she would say, shaking her head. Tiredness; both she and her mother were consumed by it. Both early risers with demanding jobs, they liked nothing better than to collapse in a chair and have a power nap or 'shut eye' as it was known when her mother worked, to recharge the batteries and unwind.

Sometimes she felt like her mother when she bent down to pick up bits off the floor or the stairs, maybe a shred of paper torn when opening a letter, or toast crumbs, dropped on the way from the kitchen to the sitting room without a plate or grass brought in from the garden and thoughtlessly walked through the house. Or if there was an unfamiliar mark on the carpet which had not been there the last time she walked across it. She would bend down and scratch it with her finger. She knew by the size of the stride that someone had not taken their trainers off at the door. The children were good, their friends had to be treated like them and they too had to remove their trainers. It was an unspoken rule and even though the children and their friends were all grown up, they still remove their trainers. She remembered her mother finding an unfamiliar mark on her new carpet in front of the fire, not obvious but it was there, camouflaged in the pattern, she bent over and rubbed the mark with her bitten thumb. It was a burn and it had singed and melted a neat brown circle in the pile. All hell was let loose. She shouted and complained that she had scrimped and saved to have something nice and that nobody cared less. Her mother had blamed her and she protested saying that it wasn't her and that she hadn't touched the fire and didn't smoke anyway. She was sure it was her father but couldn't prove it and he did not own up. She was not believed, and later, when she tried her key in the lock, she found that she couldn't get in. She had been locked out. In her own home they had terrific fires, fires that sometimes burnt all night and didn't need lighting in the morning. The heat was intense; crackling wood and spitting coal sent sparks flying and she too was concerned about the carpet and put an off cut down to protect.

Sparks would travel quite a distance and land on her skirt or a cushion, making a perfect hole. She would jump up and brush her hand across her lap or shake the cushion; too late of course. The acrid smell of burning wool was left hanging in the air. Besides being a constant source of heat, the fire was alive. A little boy came round once to play with her son. He had never seen a fire before and sat by the hearth until his mother came to pick him up two hours later. He was totally mesmerized, watching the flames leap and dance, flickering, and besides the ordinary yellow and orange flames there were spurts of pink and purple and jets of green showering beads of coloured light. The coal split into crevices, fresh smoke and then once it got going a flame, on, off, on, off, like a light switch until there was enough momentum to burst, full of life, casting light and shadows. The fire was the hub, the focal point in the house from October to April. The coalmen brought the black glistening fossils in sacks over their shoulders and tipped them into the concrete coal bunker by the back gate. She always had to remove the lid ready for the men. They wore brown leather jerkins to protect their bodies from the weight and with one swinging movement tipped out the coal. She could feel the vibration where she stood in the kitchen and she knew to count to ten. It was a comforting feeling having a coal bunker full of coal. It was like having a sack of potatoes; no need to worry about warmth or food for at least a month. The wrought iron grate was made locally to accommodate the wide hearth and two fire bricks were positioned at each end to reduce the amount of coal used. Somehow she had never quite got round to having a coal scuttle and a companion set, the fireplace accessories, and instead used a galvanised bucket to carry the coal to the grate and a small spade and a brush with nylon bristles which gradually melted to half the length.

Laying the fire was a labour of love. Raked first thoroughly with the poker, the grey ash forming a soft dune under the grate, sheets of newspapers squeezed into balls and sticks laid crisscross fashion, striking the match and igniting the paper here and there until it whooshed into flames, sparks snapping and flying. Placing the coal, the flames choked, smoke enveloping, curling like a black veil, being drawn upwards. Reappearing, the flames would blink in and out until they took hold, licking, excited, until they settled burning red and hot, warmth filling the room, so warm that it sapped and drained. Even Charlie, her dog, would take himself off into a cool corner and collapse like a marionette. Anything thrown on it sizzled, spat and melted, consumed in the volcanic heat. Plates were scraped, crisp bags thrown, shrunk to the size of a first-class stamp, a chicken carcase reduced to dust, its smell permeating the night air. Apple tree prunings would scent the air, an ancient woodland smell. In the morning, when the fire was cold and spent and no longer had the energy to support itself, the cobbles relaxed and settled, air and ash hung firmly together, like a piece of fine art that people would pay to see, an illusion. The fire came into its own on Christmas Eve, the one night in the year when having a chimney was essential. Father Christmas called and made a right mess, leaving footprints in the ash on the hearth and on the carpet, and although he had drunk his sherry (must have been thirsty) he didn't eat all of his mince pie. He had taken one bite and left it (must have been fed up with mince pies). He read the letters left on the mantelpiece by her four children and put presents in the socks and the pillowslips placed around the room. Father Christmas had hardly picked up the reins "Now, Dasher! Now, Dancer! Now, Prancer and Vixen! On, Comet! On Cupid! On, Donner and Blitzen!" half asleep, the children crept downstairs and quietly opened the door. They were so excited. They could see from the mess in the hearth that Father Christmas had come and that their wishes had been granted. She wondered what it was like in homes where there were no fireplaces, or dirty black chimneys. Did people leave their back doors open? She was glad that she had had a real fire when her children were small; much more fun. She remembered the fire when she was small. Her mother had the chore of lighting the fire first thing in the morning and to ensure that it would light she dolloped copious amounts of floor polish on the sticks. It clung thickly, there was no way that it wouldn't burn when the match was struck. If there was a time when the fire was having difficulty drawing, she would kneel down in front of the fire and open out the pages of The Daily Telegraph and hold them flush against the tile surround allowing the air to whoosh up from the ash pan. She didn't have a coal scuttle or a companion set either, like her, she just made do.

The fire – as she knew it – ended with the mother of all fires. She could hear a frightening roar high above, in the chimney breast. She ran outside. Flames leapt from the chimney in the bright February afternoon. She called to her husband who was busy in the garden, ran in and dialled 999. Holding a towel round each end, she and her husband picked up the grate, full of licking, burning coal and got it outside. Where did that inner strength come from? It must have weighed a ton. She had never been able to budge the grate for twenty years. She was frightened. Her long hair hung over, dangerously close to the flames. Her heart was pounding. She was weak with fear. Doors open, the firemen were everywhere. They rushed through the house with their hoses, damping down. They were in the loft checking the brickwork and on the roof checking the chimney.

They still had fires but the outdoor variety. In the autumn, when the air was still, her husband would have a bonfire to burn the debris and rubbish that had accumulated over the growing season. After checking for hedgehogs he would douse the fire with petrol and step back and throw a lighted match. She heard the bang and felt it too, she knew what he had done. She would run upstairs and look out of the window. In the dark she could see the fire leaping out of the big rusty oil drum and her husband's shadow leaning on his fork watching the fire. The most recent outdoor fire was the Mexican chimenea, imported like everything else from China. When she had been in Tarragona she had seen China Shipping stamped on the sides of containers bound for Europe. While she and her husband had been away during the Christmas holidays her children had had great fun outside until the early hours getting drunk and stoking the chimera. But the other day, when her son had popped home briefly her husband said, "Let's get the 'chim' going." Her son loved the fire just as much as her husband; it held a fascination. Really, her husband wanted to hold the poker, to be in charge and place the logs, but he let go and let his son do it. Only a few times did he intervene. He couldn't help himself. Her son was left handed and he held the poker in his left hand. He pulled his chair forward, scraping the legs on the loose gravel. He leaned forward to move and adjust the logs and twigs to get the best glow and the most warmth. Ash dispersed on the warm rising air.

She remembered finding inner strength when she was helping her husband lift an RSJ into position in the dining room, the same room as the fire had been. Two steel joists were welded together to form a T shape constructed to support the rooms upstairs. Stretched to her limit she never knew how she got her end onto the brick pillar. She, like her mother, was determined.

It dawned on her, as she scrawled the address on her nephew's birthday card, that her hand writing was like her mother's. She shaped her letters in the same way, relaxed and free, no particular form. When she left a note on the kitchen table for anyone who cared to read it: 'If it stops raining please hang the washing out or put the chicken in the oven at no. 5 at 2 30pm. Love mum.' It was the 'mum' that looked so like her mother's. In fact, you could only tell the first m then it dissolved into a wavy line. Ss too were careless, scribbled almost. Her mother was a stickler for words spelt correctly and would tell you straight away, almost hurtfully, if there was a mistake, making you feel demoralised and uncomfortable. Even thank you letters from her grandchildren were not spared.

Sometimes she found herself doing similar things, like idly folding or pleating a napkin or hem of her skirt, then smoothing it flat, then doing it again, vaguely aware that it was an 'old person's' habit. In her mind however, she was practising the technical process and therefore it was justified. In her mind she was matching the loose threads of the tailor tacks and top stitching as close as she dared to the fold, back stitching at the end to secure the knife pleat in position. For her this was not unusual. She was always making things in her mind or working out how things were made, unpicking things and putting them together again.

When she bit into a slice of buttered toast and rested it on her plate to sip her tea, her bite was the same as her mother's. Her mother was proud that she still had some of her own teeth. Although she had tried, she had never managed to get used to false teeth with their bright pink gums and bright white teeth. Gradually her own teeth had fallen into disrepair and some she had swallowed, leaving the metal posts to rub. Lack of N.H.S. dentists were in the news, again. Connie's mind went back to when she was small. When her tooth was wobbly, she had a piece of cotton thread wrapped around and around the tooth. The other end of the thread was tied to the door handle. Her father closed the door. Or, he fetched the pliers from the electric box and roughly gripped her tooth and pulled. The dentist in Kingsway was vivid in her mind. A frightening place. The gas bottles standing around like old petrol pumps. The hostile equipment waiting on the green glass tray. The hideous black rubber mask placed over her nose, pressing herself into the green reclining chair until overcome by the halothane, she dreamed of rabbits. Whenever her dentist of thirty-five years looked at her teeth reflected in the mouth mirror she was reminded of that awful experience. Upper left, eight missing, seven present, watch the occlusal, six present, mesial drift, five missing, space reduced, four present and so on. Her children used to play dentists on her upright vacuum cleaner. They used to lean on the upright part and be lowered into position. Then the 'dentist' would check their teeth and give them a badge.

Her mother loved her bed. She loved the thick, warm, dopey feeling. She cuddled a hot water bottle, covered in a furry feel. She would fill it long before going to bed and wrap her nightdress around it. The bottle smelt densely of feet and rubber, a heavy, choking combination. Although it warned on the neck of the bottle, do not fill with boiling water, she always did, clicking the switch on the kettle over and over just to make sure that it was. It was still frothing and bubbling as she poured. Concentrating, she would squeeze the bottle against her bosom to release any air and fasten with the rubber stopper, turning tightly. She would then shake the bottle upside down over the kitchen sink to release any surplus water, then take the tea towel and mop up the water around the stopper. Once, she forgot the stopper, the boiling water erupted, cascading all over her, scalding, burning, blistering tender skin. A nurse came in to dress the inflamed weeping flesh just as she had done when a pot of boiling rice pudding spilt over her arms, removing the skin, exposing fresh raw, wet, glistening tissue. She too liked a hot water bottle but not while her husband was there to snuggle into. But sometimes she did feel like her mother or imagined that she looked like her, when she closed her eyes and dented the pillow. She would look like her when she went to sleep for the last time. Her once golden hair, grey and thin, her pink scalp clearly visible. Her skin slipping over her bones. Thank goodness for the creeping dark.

She was fully aware of her family traits and at times felt compelled to do the opposite or contradict what she had been used to, to improve or do away with bad habits like a comb in the kitchen or hoarding junk mail. She would have her name and address torn off, shredded and the contents recycled pronto. Unlike her mother, she would file documents regularly, in order, therefore easy to find and refer to. She was never a slave to her kitchen floor or the windows, forever cleaning and getting upset if they got dirty. Once a year suited her and if she missed a year, well so what? At least she didn't leave half empty jam pots in the cupboard to grow mould, or close the curtains before it was dark. In her dreams she and her mother were the same person.

***

She had seen him look in the case before. He had been so engrossed that he had not noticed her. She always wondered what was so interesting in it. He would get on his hands and knees. He would huff and puff because of his big hard stomach. He would pull out the case and lift it onto the bed. Slowly he would get to his feet and snap it open. He kept money in it, lots of money, in neat bundles. He would look at it and pick the bundles up, thumbing the notes, enjoying the feel, rearranging, checking, then close the lid again and return the case to its place next to the china pot full to the brim of acrid yellow water. Years later, the Bank of England changed the design of the five pound note and all of his five hundred pounds were out of date, discovered purely by chance when his wife was out shopping and the cashier refused to accept a five pound note for the newspaper. She knew nothing about her father, nothing that she had actually been told. Many times she might have guessed but in her teens she decided to see for herself what was in the case and satisfy her curiosity, and just like him, on her hands and knees, lifted the green slippery counterpane that covered her parents' bed. Prying into something that was clearly nothing to do with her made her feel dishonest, but her anticipation and excitement got in the way of morals and when the coast was clear she carefully slid out the case.

The dark brown case was small. It measured 10x16x 4 and although it didn't have real leather stamped anywhere, it clearly was. The handle also made of leather, top stitched as the whole case was in thick cotton thread. In small gold lettering was the name of the craftsmen, John Pound and Co Ltd London, imprinted inside the lid. Her mother must have bought the case as a present, because he would not have bought one of such good quality. It had become scratched and marked with time but that simply just added to its intrigue. Opening it, she found that the lid was divided into many sections, each filled with pieces of paper, envelopes, newspaper cuttings and of course the money, neatly lining the main part of the case. She thought that she might come across something interesting like her birth certificate or photographs of her parents wedding. No; there had been nothing to stir her emotions. Leaving the contents exactly as she had found them, she closed the case. She found the contents of the case to be much more interesting forty years later. Of course the money had gone, but the carefully preserved memorabilia were still there, untouched.

She didn't recognize the man in the brown leather case as being her father. The fading yellow newspaper articles and snippets neatly cut out and saved, revealed nothing other than the 'keep the spirits up' reporting from around the world during the Second World War. Most of the pieces had a link to his own regiment of which he was obviously immensely proud. A picture from The Illustrated War News 1915 showed a picture of Highlanders charging at Balaclava in 1854. Had he kept that picture since he was thirteen? The classic military painting was housed in Stirling Castle, the base for his regiment, The Argyll and Sutherland Highlanders. Google did a search and found the painting. On the computer screen it was small and did not satisfy. She needed to see the real painting for herself, to smell the earth and see the blood and hear the cries. She would have to go to Stirling Castle. Years ago, it probably hung in a draughty room but now it was in the museum dedicated to the regiment. It was as big as her kitchen window and she stood back to observed the scene at Balaclava. The gilt frame led you into battle and held you there. She saw the terror and frightened look in the soldiers' eyes as the Russians galloped towards them on horseback, but their bayonets were fixed and determined, buttons glinting on their red jackets, sporrans flying. A grey in the foreground buckled and confusion ensued. The Thin Red Line charged forward, face to face with death, blood thirsty, stabbing and shooting as they went, vengeful, killing and maiming, fearless. Maybe her father wanted that power and glory for himself. Did he yearn to be brave and courageous like those heroes thirty years earlier? Was it a boyhood dream?

A colour reproduction of the same picture remained hanging on a wall where there had been a German raid on Ramsgate, demolishing the whole building except the wall where it hung. Rome Greets the Argylls, "this intrepid battalion of fearless Scottish warriors will take its place among the battalions who have fought so valiantly and with such insatiable tenacity under the command of the eighth," and a report dated 6th March 1943 in a magazine called 'Illustrated': "Now the pipers played their own regiment out of Malaya. The morning sun was already hot when the still air was broken by A Hundred Pipers and Hielan Laddie and the remnant Highlanders, with steady bearing and their heads high, marched from a lost campaign into a doomed island. The broad causeway was blown behind them. Malaya was lost, but no one would have guessed it from the tunes that the pipers played. The future was darker than a winter storm, but the 93rd marched against it to a vaunting triumphal music. The motto of the battalion was Sans Peur. Her father had never given any indication of being proud and loyal. She never remembered him being passionate and pleased with anything, other than himself. He wore his full walking-out uniform on Hogmanay.

He wore the full regalia, as her mother called it, the tam-o-shanter, the badge polished, the grosgrain ribbons flying down the back but also stitched neatly round the edge holding the distinctive red and white checked knitting firmly in place, the small red pom-pom, completely concealed until the bonnet was opened out and positioned on his thinning hair, the knee length socks with garters and colours, the cuffs turned, hiding the elastic. The badger on the sporran facing death again, eyes bright, the rough hair smooth. Six tassels made out of hair, covered with brass caps and beautifully decorated with thistles, swung as he walked. The sporran was backed in red leather and concealed a wallet fastened with a brass button; the ultimate man bag. The kilt was heavy and made of wool. It was tight and taught across his expanding waistline. Where the pleats were stitched, the kilt was lined with coarse, natural coloured blanket, rough and itchy and stamped like a sack or a sheep, with H&SH. She remembered rough itchy blankets that used to be her Grandma's that were passed on, eventually to her and when worn out and thin, she had made them into a Victorian peasant costume, tied with string, for her son's school trip to Holdenby House. Her father wore the full regalia with a green Harris tweed jacket and of course a shirt and tie. She came across a small square black and white photo of herself when she was two holding her father's hand. He was wearing the entire ensemble on a warm sunny day. On Hogmanay, when he had been all fired up with alcohol, he would sing songs and ballads, learnt off by heart and never forgotten, from his army days. He would sing "Bless this House", loving the applause and attention that everyone gave him, smiling a slimy smile, showing his gold tooth. Slime and smile, same word really.

How times have changed, for the better thank God, especially for women. In another article, neatly cut out and folded in half a retired county court judge gives his advice to young men. "When you begin walking out with a girl the very first time look at her eyes and see whether they are warm, bright and kind or whether they are catty. If they are catty, sheer off. Beware of the saintly woman, the woman who spends her life in church. Saints are wonderful, although they may be rather difficult for sinners to live with. The wife who is always wanting to reform one can be very trying. Beware too, of the amusement fan. The wife who is always wanting to go to dances, however tired you are, can be very trying. Beware of the stupid woman, for marriage with a fool, however sweet and lovely she may be, is a drab affair for the cleverer partner, and she will give him stupid children." Now this was much more like the father she knew, patronizing and humiliating her mother and his daughters at every opportunity, treating his family to his coarse army ways, making them jump to attention, commanding respect, making everyone's life a misery, just for his own gratification.

The artefacts in the case hinted at how the country was at the time, the war economy labels to reuse on envelopes, the clothing book of 1946/47 containing brown, lilac and quarter coupons and the fuel ration book stamped 1957. There was a stunning black and white photograph torn out of the 1950 British Journal Photographic Almanac, of a beautiful woman in a checked grosgrain taffeta skirt tied with a cummerbund, sultry Elizabeth Taylor eyes and wearing a turban, her bare breasts neat and pert, looked at she supposed, to rouse and inflame his desire. His passport with the foreign office stamp pressed into it, dated 1949. As far as she knew he had not been abroad. She decided to drive north and check out the addresses that she had found crossed out and redirected and a small square photograph of a little boy. Not discouraged, she had phoned her friend one Sunday and put it to her, "What about driving to Scotland?"

Unlike the journey fifty years ago it was easy. They chatted all the way and when they didn't, they felt comfortable with that too. They didn't notice the relentless traffic thin out, the scenery changing, great bold shapes heaving out of the ground, defiant and proud, filling the sky. Swollen streams seeped into the fields, smudging the banks, in a hurry to get to the sea. The two of them went over and over how it was or imagining how it might have been back in 1946. She had had visions of drab grey houses merging with low cloud, and drizzle. People out only to do the messages, as they say and get some shopping. She had seen Scotland like that, wet slates, pavements gleaming and reflecting, the atmosphere heavy and waterlogged. It wasn't like that, it was sunny and bright and although the houses were grey, or stippled and painted, they did not look drab. The once council-owned properties looked cared for, gardens tended, hedges cut. The first address had been demolished and a new house was being built where there was a gap. At the second address there was no reply when she knocked. She asked a woman walking her dog if she knew of the woman who had once lived there. She could see her thinking, then she suggested speaking to her friend who lived two houses away. The two women exchanged thoughts and suggested that she went to the bowling club behind the church. She thanked the women for their help and crossed the road with her friend. The bowling green grass was like felt and cut with precision. The whole area was neat, with wooden seats at intervals allowing spectators to watch. They were being watched as they approached the pavilion in the corner. Hesitantly, she opened the door and enquired after this woman. At least half a dozen women all older than them, wanted in and threw ideas about, not afraid to snitch on anyone, not afraid to divulge secrets, loving the attention of the two Sassenachs from down south. One woman grabbed the phonebook from the glass topped table by the door and thumbed through the pages to check a number, suggesting that this person might be able to help with her enquiry. In the noisy confusion she calmly wrote down a telephone number and a different address. They thanked the ladies of the bowling club for their help and they said their goodbyes.

She drove round to Prince Avenue to the tenement opposite the Spar. The front of the tenements looked reasonably respectable but the backs retained their forbidding look. The upper floors were reached by metal stairs and narrow paths connected the warren. The outside toilets built opposite the back doors were now used for storage and the washing lines reached out, connecting the communities. In the past it must have been squalid with the overcrowding, the dirt, the lack of sanitation. That was life then and you just got on with it. She walked through an alley to the back of the building and climbed two flights of concrete stairs. She could see the name carved in a wooden plaque beside the front door. She was not afraid or nervous, she was only going to say hello and satisfy her curiosity. She knocked and a cheery woman opened the door. She wore glasses and her hair was silver grey and curled. She wore a white knitted top and an apron over her flowery skirt. As briefly as possible she explained the purpose of the visit. "And who wants to know?" she asked. She had to be honest, there was no point in being otherwise and replied that she thought that she was a relation. She turned round and went back along the carpeted hall, leaving her standing at the door.

She reappeared, "You'd better come in." She followed her through to the living room " Here, take a seat". She sat down on the settee beside Gordon. He was quiet and gentle, his eyes clear and blue. His father was her father. Gordon was her half brother and he went on to say that he was the youngest of eight children when his father, her father, disappeared in 1946, leaving his wife to cope and bring up the children on her own. Gordon had been thirteen, the youngest. Joan, his wife, was excitable, asking questions, getting the facts straight, repeating herself, fond of Gordon's mother. She talked too much. She tore a piece of lined A4 paper out of an exercise book and made a list of Gordon's brothers and sisters and beside their names a list of all their children. Gordon discouraged her from including the next generation, implying that there were plenty of names already. Joan made tea and buttered slices of home made fruit loaf, very welcome and much needed. Two pieces of toast at seven o'clock seemed a long way off. Gordon was reserved and wanted to ask her more. "Have you got a family?" She was confused and didn't immediately understand what he meant and he repeated the question. Of course, she had four sons. Joan found two photos of her mother-in-law, one on her own and one with Gordon, Joan and their daughter, Linda, with her husband. Gordon loved his mother, "The best you could get."

The family must have known that her father was still somewhere when the solicitor called at Margaret's house in 1980 with divorce papers. She wanted to see a photograph of Gordon's mother when she was young. She wanted to compare her with her own mother. She showed Gordon the photo of the boy. He had no idea who he was. The image that Gordon conveyed of her father was the same as hers, that he had had a high opinion of himself. She told him that he had worked until retiring age and even continued with part time jobs for pocket money. There was really nothing much to tell that she wanted to share with her new-found relations. Joan revelled in the fact that they would be talk of the town and she knew that the phone would be red hot as soon as they left. How had her father the nerve to say to her boyfriend in 1968 that if he had had sons he would have wanted them to go in the army? He had four sons. Not satisfied with the revelation of eight half brothers and sisters, they drove the next morning to check out the third address. She parked outside and knocked on the door. No reply. She sat in the car again to think. The angle of the wooden blinds in the front window tilted. Someone was in. She went to the back door and knocked. "Mrs Galbraith, next door will be able to help you." Indeed she did. She knew the names of tenants right back to the fifties; Mr and Mrs McKay, Mr Craig, and Mr and Mrs Stewart but unfortunately they were not the names that she wanted to hear. Having called at the third address and drawn a blank she decided to retrace her steps much nearer to home to an address on a redirected letter dated 1946.

She went to Berkhamstead, the nearest small town in Hertfordshire, to check all the telephone directories in the area where they used to work after the war. She went upstairs to the reference section and unlike her library at home, there was an array of floppy directories all leaning against each other. The Hemel Hempstead directory was on the top shelf and distinctly marked reference. She looked up the name. There was nothing. She scanned through St Albans, Watford, Slough; nothing. Some were brand new, their thin pages still pressed together with the force of the guillotine when they were trimmed into books. She went back to the Hemel Hempstead copy and looked up Abbots Hill. It was still a school. She was surprised seeing it there in black and white and made a note of the number. It was the school where her parents had worked. She presumed that it might have changed its use over the years to a conference centre or an old peoples home, but no. Her mother had known this area well and years ago, when she had taken her mother with her to collect her son from the Reading Festival, she recalled place names and people from the distant past. She was so near, she would check the map. She had visions of the school set in its own grounds surrounded by woods and fields and kept away from the town centre signs. Suddenly, there was the name attached to a real sign post, so small she really wondered if she had seen it at all. She turned immediately left. There it was, a grand sign set up high and commanding, important. There was a gatehouse on the left. She followed the narrow leafy road, she drove on and the house appeared on the side of the hill, grey stone and majestic, like Manderlay in Rebecca. To her the house did not seem unfamiliar. It was as she had imagined, she had been before. She parked. Smart dark green signs directed her to the reception. The hefty oak door, like one for a church or a castle was open and she walked in, there were workmen around, glass partitions divided the once big rooms into offices. The secretary in the main office asked how she could help. Briefly, she explained and the secretary found another woman who asked if she would like to be shown around. She was amazed at being allowed for such a flimsy reason, and the fact that Maggie had given up her time to do so. They sat on a cushioned window seat in the dining room overlooking the grounds and the valley beyond. It was now a day school for girls but in her mother's day it had been a ladies finishing school for boarders. The school had been undergoing a major change in order to keep up with the times. The girls had come from wealthy families, and even abroad and until quite recently, kept to its traditional values. Its comfortable ease was everywhere. It was old and worn and such a stark contrast to the school where she was a teacher.

They walked round the whole building, even into the basement where the old electric meters had just been removed, exposing the original brick housing and a gleaming new tardis stood in the corner. Would that withstand the next hundred years? There was a chapel, which sadly had been reduced in size to accommodate new offices, its walls panelled as so much of the interior of the house was, and brass plaques dedicated to past pupils and teachers. She had seen the names in a small prospectus belonging to her mother which she had come across in a pile of photos. Names like Dolores and Belinda and double barrelled names, common in those days in wealthy families, unlike today when divorce or living together has become the norm. She went where her mother had walked and worked and slept. Her mother's maiden name was in the prospectus under the heading Cook-Housekeeper. A little while later a large white envelope arrived, an A4 document about Abbots Hill in war-time. The accounts of past pupils described their experiences. Further on, there was an interesting paragraph; it was from Mrs Prescott, " I do not remember exactly when it was we had a new cook. She absolutely revolutionized the kitchen's approach to food. She was Scottish, with honey coloured hair pinned in a loose bun and had a lovely round face. She always thought of us as her poor bairns that needed feeding, rather than just the utter nuisances we felt we were before! Every meal was better, and she actually asked us whether we had enjoyed this and that and beamed when we said we had done. On Sundays, she somehow managed to squeeze just that tiny bit more out of our rations and make everyone a little cake each for tea. This was a treat beyond belief." This was her mother. She had never in her life heard her mother use the word bairns.

Her father's name was not recorded but she knew that he had worked there because the headmistress had written a reference which praised his good character, describing him as reliable, trustworthy, hard working, conscientious and exemplary, hand written in ink. Well, exemplary he was not. This was the address that a letter had been redirected to in 1947, but it had not been forwarded by Margaret, it had been sent by someone else. Maybe this was where the small black and white photograph of the boy had come from. Maybe there was another son. She felt sure that there was. Joan, too, was curious and contacted her sister-in-law. Apparently, while Margaret was away with friends, her husband, (her father) had cleared out their furniture and set up home with another woman and Douglas. Well now she knew the name, the D in the savings book discovered in the brown leather case was for Douglas. She logged on. The search on the internet brought up fifty eight people with that name. Throwing caution to the wind she registered to find out more. She scrolled through the names. There it was, just the name without any dates but someone called Jennifer also wanted to know about him. Intrigued, she sent a message. Having always refused to get swept along with technology, she was suddenly looking in the inbox and checking her Emails.

Somerset house as she knew it had gone; it was now a restaurant and gallery. She had been there once when her first son was born to check her own birth certificate. She remembered carrying him in the blue canvas sling, and finding somewhere to feed him had been impossible. Her birth certificate had said 1965. Maybe her mother had lost the original, or thrown it away with the rubbish hoarded in the drawers. Her new birth certificate showed that she was born in The Haven, Yateley, but in column five it said her mother's maiden name followed by her married name. How could she have said that she was married when clearly she wasn't? She looked again at her parents' marriage certificate. They were married on the 15th May 1980 and looking at the handwriting, even the signatures, the whole document was written by the same person.

She typed in The Haven, Yateley, and there it was, the place where she was born. Why had she not looked before? The photographs showed the garden and the front of the house, the rattan chairs, piled in the corner waiting for endless summer days. She had a small photo of her mother holding her, days old, wrapped in a shawl with those rattan chairs stacked higgledy-piggledy in the corner. Taking photographs at the mother and baby home had been forbidden, although, as Valerie Kerslake of The Yateley Society wrote, some mothers contrived to do so, including her mother. Her mother's face looked smooth and young. There was a softness and she was smiling. She looked fondly at her daughter. The photo had been taken from the side and you could not see her brown eyes. Her profile was the same as her daughter's now, her deep forehead and thin pointed nose, her jaw sharp. Her dark auburn hair swept up and back in a bun at the nape of her neck, two tortoiseshell combs taming the escaping wisps at her temples. Her clothes were good and underneath her dark wool crepe dress she wore a cream blouse buttoned to the neck. She cradled her tiny daughter, her perfect soft downy head resting in the crook of her mother's arm. Her right arm rested over the shawl. She would never know what she thought or how she felt. She couldn't ask her now. It was too late.

Her daughter had never known that there was anything to ask about. Contact with the babies was discouraged. Even bathing and changing them was not allowed. After three or four weeks, bottle feeding replaced breast feeding, so reducing the bond. Fifty years ago there was 'immense shame' to conceiving a child outside marriage, not only for the girl but her family as well. For most girls, adoption was their only choice, as bringing up a child alone was difficult without support from the father or her own family. The girls were encouraged to write to their families and tell them of the baby's birth. Her mother told no one. Some girls, like her mother, however, did keep their babies. Reading further, "one girl knew from the moment she saw her little daughter that she could never let her go." Years ago her mother would recall hearing the cuckoo on that April morning. It had been glorious. Sun poured in through the mullioned windows casting warmth and bands of light across the scrubbed wooden floorboards. Windows were thrown open to let in the soft spring air. Lying there, confined to bed, listening to the birds chattering, she felt fresh and alive. The awful experience of giving birth over and the elation that followed blotted out the insecurity of the future. She knew that it would take a long time to claw back that respectability that she once had. In her scrawled handwriting on the back of the photo her mother had written 'Constance and her mum' and obviously sent it to her father. It was found in his brown leather case in one of the pockets. Before that, it might have been kept in a wallet because one edge was soft and worn.

She phoned her local office for births deaths and marriages. The lady was helpful and gave her the telephone number. The office in Edinburgh sent her the form and she ticked the relevant boxes.

The letter had come in the post. She had been expecting it. When she opened the front door, her eyes darted to the stairs, where the mail accumulated, scanning to see if a letter, self addressed to her had arrived. She would have recognised her own handwriting at a glance, and the fold in the middle of the envelope. It was there. The letter was there. She waited and went through the house and into the garden, delaying and putting off what she might find. She collected the washing from the line and filled the kettle then she went to the stairs and picked up the letter. Folded inside was a copy of Douglas's birth certificate. His father was her father and Douglas's mother was called Dorothy but had the same surname. She was an insurance agent.

How could they have been married when her father was already married to Margaret? On the certificate Dorothy's signature does not look confident. It looked suspiciously as though she was going to write something else then corrected it. After receiving the birth certificate she knew that she would have to go back and asked her friend to join her once again. They returned in the next half term.

She parked right outside the post office in Main Street, went in and asked the young man where Cadden Lea was. Not surprisingly, he hadn't a clue and she crossed over to the Crown Hotel. She and her friend went into the saloon bar. It was sparse and empty. The young barman asked what they would like, and they replied that they would like to speak to some local people, preferably old local people and were there any in the public bar next door? Indeed, there were, and the two women wove their way around the empty tables and chairs through to the public bar and sat with their drinks on a long reddish vinyl seat against a blank beige wall. The handful of early evening drinkers turned to look at them. The public bar was basic, the chairs lacked comfort and were devoid of any style. It was all a bit stark, laid out more like a waiting room. The fluorescent atmosphere resembled a fifties milk bar. They looked at each other and moved in towards the three old boys. 'Do you mind if we join you?' said her friend, placing her drink on the table. The youngest old man, the man with the toupee, wanted to know if the women were from the Inland Revenue or the DHSS, he reckoned that they were nosey enough. They said that they were from neither but he was not convinced. It had never crossed her mind that anyone would think such a thing. How odd. Except for Bob, the men were in their sixties and knew all the comings and goings in the village. Between them they knew whom to ask and where to source information. The man wearing the wig got up and moved over to the bar, picked up the mobile phone and the mini local directory, a handy booklet that cost a pound, the proceeds of which went to the community hall fund. He checked a number and made a call. Once it was ringing he handed the phone to her and she had this strange conversation with Marjory about Cadden Lea and how in 1947 it was owned by a family called Blair and that it had been used as a boarding house, let out to the officers' wives who were visiting their husbands stationed in the village.

The old boys were celebrating Bob's seventy-fifth birthday. They didn't look as though they needed an excuse to celebrate. The whiskey was flowing and the pints followed. Glasses littered the small square table that they shared. It was wet with slops and spills, the beer mats inadequate. The men seemed to treat the bar as an extension to their homes. It would not have surprised her to see carpet slippers under the table. As it was their appearance was casual, bordering on untidy; jogging bottoms and quilted jerkins. The man on the right held a roll-up between his fingers. His nails were dirty, he sipped his whiskey and drew on his cigarette. A few moments later he exhaled like a twin exhaust. Smoke clouded the celebration. He seemed oblivious, such was the intensity of the pleasure. Even by six o'clock they were plastered, their tongues were loose and their words slurred. There had been a number of boarding houses in the village, used to accommodating the transient population. It had earned itself the nickname of Tinkertown. Gypsies, too, would come to the village and live on the common in tents and vans. Within a week of war being declared, the village was inundated with ninety evacuees, and a month later, more arrived to swell the growing population. There were so many children that the local children went to school in the morning and the evacuees in the afternoon. In 1941 Thornhill was declared an official rest centre in the event of severe bombing in Scotland. The village was awash with soldiers and army personnel. The Cheshire regiment was billeted in the village and the local hotels were used to house the troops. The old boys dispersed for their suppers, a little unsteady on their feet and their faces red and blotchy in the harsh lighting.

The village was larger and busier than expected. The main road climbed slowly to the 'cross' where it dropped down to Common land. The houses hugged the kerb and most were small and low, just two windows either side of the front door. They were not bungalows. That description belonged to new housing stock, no these were old, originally weavers' cottages and although tidy, and even painted white and primrose, some looked sadly dingy and neglected. Thornhill had been a thriving weaving community but its flourishing industry began to decline as factories began making textiles.

She stood in the sitting room, she didn't move from the mat at the front door. Cadden Lea had been a weaver's cottage. The small rooms were filthy. They were cramped and overcrowded. A hundred years ago, the weavers were poor and complained bitterly about their appalling conditions; the earth floors, the damp, the lack of sanitation. This was where Douglas's mother had lived. This was the address on his birth certificate. Casting her eyes around the sitting room, the freshly painted walls, the smell of newly fitted carpet, the dust covers over the furniture, pictures waiting to be hung, it was hard to imagine the squalor and deprivation that was so common in isolated rural communities. The cottage was no longer named Cadden Lea, but number thirty seven.

While she was there she remembered that the Falkirk Herald used to arrive regularly when she was small. She never thought anything about it; it was just a newspaper and it came in the post, rolled up and fastened with a piece of brown paper around the middle. Her father would sit in his armchair, a cigarette on his lip, ash defying gravity and hanging on until its length became too much and broke off, crumbling into dust, peppering his tie and his trousers. He would brush it with the back of his hand, smudging and knowing that his wife would be displeased. He would read the paper from cover to cover, engrossed, his eyes searching and scanning the columns for something familiar. She knew now that he would have been looking for something, maybe hoping to read about his children or his wife. He must have read about his children getting married and the births of his grandchildren. She wondered who had sent the paper. Could it have been Dorothy or was it someone else?

After the excellent journey, the weather changed. The murky grey afternoon at Stirling Castle gave way to relentless rain, lashing spiteful rain, the wipers barely keeping up with the torrent. Black branches grabbed and clawed at her little car in the narrow lanes. Leaves were torn off the trees and hurtled to the ground, sodden and heavy. The clocks had changed and the evening drew in early. A steady stream of headlights made their way home. Her vision blurred from the spray thrown up by the tyres. Everything wet and streaming. Distorted ribbons of coloured light zipping past. She and her friend found their hotel and checked in, and unlike the previous visit, were early enough to have a meal instead of walking along the road cradling a portion of chips from the local chip shop, excellent though they were.

The blustery weather continued. Standing in the poly tunnel at Dunipace Mill the next morning, the rain was ferocious, the noise deafening. How could the trays of winter pansies look so cheery? The owner of the garden centre must have heard the car draw up and stop. She stood, clad in her padded, sleeveless jacket and her trousers tucked into Wellingtons. She showed her the black and white pictures that she had found in her father's brown leather case of the mill and the delivery trucks, laden with bulging sacks of grain and flour and the mill workers posing, looking directly at the camera, one foot on the running step and a bent elbow resting in the space where the window would have been, dressed in overalls and flat caps. She was obviously far too young to remember the pictures but she went indoors to fetch her father. Like his daughter he had a nice warm smile and was pleased to share the history of the mill, which as it happened, had long gone with the building of the motorway. He had had a drink. The smell clung in the damp air. Although he was older, he wasn't old enough. He recollected the fifties easily but she wanted to know about the thirties and the forties, when her father had worked at the mill. His mobile phone rang and brought the four of them back to the 21st century. Out of his breast pocket he produced the same yellow phone that her husband had. She smiled to herself. Her children referred to it as the yellow brick because of its size; one of the originals. They said their goodbyes and dashed to the car.

Joan liked keeping her informed; it made her feel important. She had extracted some more information from her sister-in-law. "When their father left and emptied the house of furniture he had gone out to a farm to work, someone told the farmer that he already had a family and he was put out and moved to Larbert." Joan also suggested that she looked on the 'Net'. So enthusiastic was she that Joan enlisted her brother to look on the 'Net' as she called it. Sure enough a family tree and a list about her father, her grandfather and her great grandfather was enclosed. Basically, they were poor, labourers, coal miners, mill workers, living in harsh conditions where the housing was poor and there was not enough money for food.

Her grandmother was a mill worker. She was called Annie. Her ill-fitting skirt was frayed and worn at the hem. It trailed in the ash that had spilled out of the range onto the bare stone floor. She sat on a low stool by the hearth. Mildew clung to the flaking wall behind her. It was dripping with condensation. Her father sat on her lap. He was the youngest of her seven sons and she supported him with her left hand, her long fingers relaxed, cradling his elbow and shoulder. The baby stared straight ahead, indifferent, his toes curled. There was a half empty feeding bottle on the range. She wore a dark plaid blouse, high at the neck, and leg of mutton sleeves pulled up above the elbow. She had a sad pensive look; her dark eyes tired, heavy with lack of sleep. She looked unhappy, subdued, her mouth set, resigned as though she had lost the will. Her hair lacked care and attention and her fringe fell in clumps on her forehead. Her husband, William, was a coal miner and they lived near the colliery. Their house was small and cramped, their furniture sparse. At the turn of the century widespread poverty and deprivation in working class areas was rife and, like the weavers' cottages in Thornhill, it must have been grim. Farmers too, experienced hardship; their cottages were long and low, built in the lee of the hill, out of the wind. The women did the backbreaking job of sowing the potatoes in drills made by the men with wooden foot ploughs, their fringed shawls crossed over their chests and fastened behind their backs, scarves around their heads. The pannier of seed potatoes was carried by the women on their backs, held by a thick leather strap across the chest, like an animal. Life was hard. The men smoked and leaned on their ploughs, the women were grimfaced, stooped, their bare hands raw and cold.

She logged on to see if anything interesting had appeared. Yes, it had. Someone called Brian knew who Douglas had married, along with a date. Once again she contacted the General Register Office in Edinburgh. This time there was nothing. She was disappointed. He hadn't got married in Scotland. Looking for Douglas had ground to a halt. Clues had come to nothing. She needed to look again, to revisit. Maybe she had missed something. She looked at the website "Falkirk Today", suggested by Joan and scrolled through the memory lane feature, scanning the names below the photos. Nothing. She left a message hoping to jog a memory. Maybe he had been adopted. Maybe he had emigrated. Lizzie at Traceline sent her some forms. She was not giving up. A letter came from Thornhill. Marjory, to whom she had spoken on the mobile in the Crown, had been asking around in the village and Douglas's mother's name had been remembered. She was back on track. With Brian's information she did a Google search for Douglas's mother. Someone else had been finding out about their family history and twelve pages appeared. She printed them all but was only interested in nine lines. Dorothy was married to James, then it listed her father as Dorothy's second husband, and their son Douglas, born in 1946. The next line was about Diane, Douglas's wife, and then the names of their three children. With all this information, she had to make progress but she didn't. She sat beside her son while he logged on to the electoral roll. There were pages of names. Where would she start? She didn't. Well she tried two, the ones with the same middle initial as Diane. Both calls failed. May and Mary were not the names she wanted to hear. She emailed Brian to see if he could add to her facts and she emailed the woman who compiled Dorothy's family tree. She wasn't very good at emailing because the postmaster replied immediately saying that it had failed.

Months later a thick, buff-coloured envelope arrived from the Historical Disclosures Office in Glasgow. She had been advised when visiting Stirling Castle to contact this office to obtain information from her father's service file. The letter included lots of useful advice and apologies about the delay because of the backlog in enquiries. To her, it seemed odd that someone had physically gone through all those dusty old yellowing files finding this and finding that so that she could piece her father's life together. She was grateful to have the information, but to her untrained eye it made hardly any sense. She half expected a timeline on a side of A4, neat and easy to read instead of pages of photocopied documents in army personnel scrawl, almost illegible, like doctors' prescriptions. With her magnifying glass in hand, she carefully read through the information, stopping when something caught her attention. The first thing to do so was a statement stating that his military conduct was exemplary. Hadn't she read that before somewhere? The army liked that word and from 1945, ATTAINED AGE 45 NO FURTHER LIABILITY FOR

RECALL was stamped across pages, but he hadn't, as her son pointed out. He wasn't forty five until 1947. Still, at last the war was over. What the heck. Addresses, now familiar, crossed out; moving on. In 1945 the testimonial reads: This NCO has been in charge of a hospital for a considerable period and I have found him to be reliable and trustworthy. At last a reference to Piper's Hill, posted there in September 1942. She was interested in Piper's Hill. She found a photograph of the big rambling house, dated on the back 1942, with nurses in starched white aprons, red crosses stamped across their chests, casualties of war seated on the bench. Safe for the time being in an English country garden. A rabbit sat on the lap of one of the nurses. She was stroking it. A moment in time. Her father stood behind the group wearing the uniform that now lay in her mother's canvas trunk. He stood upright, his hands behind his back, smiling. Going back further, he had enlisted for four years in 1931 with 7th Battalion Argyll and Sutherland Highlanders then re-engaged twice after that, until 1939 when he was posted, but it did not say where to. In December1940 he travelled south, transferring to the Royal Warwickshire Regiment. She wanted to know why. Two medals were awarded. His wife Margaret, as next of kin, was recorded, along with their eight children, born between 1920 and 1932 On the next page it clearly recalled that he was discharged from the 2nd Battalion Argyll and Sutherland Highlanders for a misstatement on enlistment, being underage at seventeen. He even said that he was married, when he didn't get married until 1920 when he was eighteen. Looking at the dates, his first baby, Mildred, was born just days after their marriage. Then she got to the page about the false information. Quite clearly he stated his year of birth as 1901 instead of 1902 Another thing, not noticed before was that he had a middle name. He called himself Jonathan Baird Weir. Maybe he said that to confuse the authorities. Indeed, his mother's maiden name was Baird and she and her sister both wore the Ancient Baird tartan but his birth certificate does not show Baird. On the next page it lists his parents, William and Annie, and his six brothers, uncles that she never knew she had: Walter, Colin, William, Samuel, George and Frederick.

Earlier that evening she had had a senior moment or rather a senior hour, surfacing from a warm deep sleep curled up on the settee only when Liverpool scored and her husband cheered. They did this three times, which was good for Liverpool, and instead of feeling tired at bedtime she was wide awake. She lay thinking about her visit to Piper's Hill. She had gone with her son. Disappointingly, the weather was dull and cold. A fine drizzle set in and the wipers were on and off. They had a spate of bad drivers on the A5, indecisive and dangerous, then overtaking just as a car approached. Disbelieving, they held their breath. They agreed that it was a useful road and that you could go anywhere on it, the Romans had the right idea, but so were the M1 and the M6 and the M25 and so it got silly. In her search for information she had come across a BBC article from the series "The People's War"; archive memories of wartime Britain. In it there was a reference to Rolls Royce and building engines during the war then it went on to talk about Freda and how she changed her job from being the stationmaster's secretary at Birmingham's New Street station to joining the Red Cross as an administrative assistant at Piper's Hill. At last, a reference to Piper's Hill, converted to a military hospital during the war. Freda Evans would be a very useful contact. She might remember her father, the man in the kilt. Freda mentioned a number of villages in the article and she jotted them down. In the road atlas they were all reasonably close to each other. They were also close to Lighthorne, where her father's mail had been redirected in 1945.

Approaching Bishops Itchington there was a sign for the post office. She turned immediately left into Chapel Street. The lady behind the counter knew exactly where she wanted to go and directed her back to the main road. She thanked her. It had been so easy and only fifty miles from home, practically on her doorstep. She indicated right and slowly drove over the cattle grid. The narrow road climbed gently to the house. Sixty years ago she knew it would have been a rough track, tyres flicking up stones. Half way up there was a farm on the left, set back. Their eyes were on the house in the foreground. Several vehicles were parked. She reversed slowly. The tyres crunched the gravel. She noticed the black kennel and in it a black dog lying down, totally ignoring the intruders. She was at the back of the house. She knocked at the main door, the door that the wounded would have been carried through on stretchers, boots noisy and people giving orders. A woman appeared at the other door, along with a tall man, not her husband, and a little boy. Already running late and needing to be on her way, the meeting was short. The house, she said had been built at the turn of the century and was still called Piper's Hill. During the war it had belonged to Col. John Lakin and The Honourable Daphne Lakin. The woman said that Daphne Lakin was still alive and must by now be in her nineties. She was very much alive according to the newspaper report only last week when she presented the trophies at a local gymkhana in Elstead, West Sussex. She had known that it had been a hospital and scrutinised the black and white photo of her house. She asked if she could walk round to the front of the house and take a photo. She replied that she was welcome to do so and to call again when she was not in such a desperate rush to leave. She and her son walked round to the front of the house overlooking the Warwickshire countryside. The clinging ivy had been removed, revealing the soft sandstone walls. The door leading onto the terrace had originally been dark and partly obscured with creepers, whereas now it was white and, suddenly, out of character. Over the years the terrace had weathered badly and needed attention. The plastic toys from Early Learning left abandoned on the fragmented terrace brought her back to reality. Their harsh colours seemed out of place, so removed from the uncertain times of 1942. The semi- circle of stone steps leading onto the lawn hadn't changed. In her picture a wooden garden seat had been placed on the steps in order to take the photograph and get everyone seated. Her son took some photos and they returned to the car. She felt as though she remembered the name Dorothy Lakin. Her father must have said it, long ago, or did she imagine that? As she seemed to remember an Uncle Sam just leaning in the doorway between the kitchen and the living room at the house where they stayed in St Andrews, when she was small. Finding Lighthorne Cottages on the Banbury Road was not so straightforward. They asked at the Antelope without success then crossed the road to the village hall, which also served as the post office. The lady suggested going back out of the village and the postman who had just pulled up said to go to the garage on the Banbury Road. In the garage the owner said that she needed to speak to the man in number two at the houses adjacent to the garage. She knocked at the door and above her the window opened. Well they were known as Lighthorne Cottages but had been renamed The Little Houses. Well, that was helpful. Once she was home she wished that she had asked about Freda.

A residential home seemed the only option left. Even with the support of various agencies, put in place by her daughter, her mother was unable to look after herself She seemed to wallow in self pity. Increasingly she would draw the curtains earlier and earlier, shutting out the world, hoping that no one would call. Not a sliver of light was allowed to intrude. When her daughter called she would be sitting in the gloom, just staring, or eyes closed, her head nodding. Ignoring the protests from her mother she would swish back the curtains, letting in the golden light, and get the kettle on. She always gave the impression that she was managing but her daughter knew that she wasn't. Even the carers were fobbed off. She would say that she had eaten breakfast and had a cup of tea when clearly she hadn't. Even at eleven o'clock the kettle was stone cold. She would be up in the night getting dressed, confused with tiredness, medication and malnutrition. She had a fall, not the first, and with what must have been immense determination, she called her daughter at one twenty two in the morning. At half past eight she listened to the messages and heard her mother's fragile voice calling for help. At eight o'clock, her carer had found her lying in a pool of blood.

Years ago, when her mother was bright and interesting, she had a noble thought of looking after her in her old age. She would feel good about that, as though she was paying back what she herself had been given. But when it came to it, she had changed and so had her mother. Somehow her mother did not fit in to her busy lifestyle and she could not have coped with her demands, mental or physical. She and her sister had talked about finding a suitable home for her but their mother had insisted that she could manage and they gave her the benefit of the doubt. She never returned to her home.

Clearing her mother's house had been a challenge. It was a job that had to be done. Dismantling her bittersweet life was unnerving, her possessions that she had scrimped and saved for, gone. It felt uncomfortable taking charge, making decisions for her about her things. There was no alternative. She and her sister looked around. They knew what was ahead of them. Daunted, they gritted their teeth and launched in, armed with rolls of industrial strength black plastic sacks. They progressed systematically, starting with the kitchen. They were ruthless. Together they held open the sack until it could support itself. Absolutely everything was removed from the cupboards and drawers. They consulted each other on each and every item, giving some a second chance before being surrendered to the black sack. Mercilessly, they continued their rampage through the house. Nothing was exempt. The bookcase was cleared, mats rolled up, clothes folded, curtains removed.

By four they were flagging. They had slowed down. They were in the main bedroom, long-abandoned by their mother. The rosy carpet had seen better days. The two small opening windows were covered with a metal mesh to discourage intruders. The window overlooked the green, which, years ago had been orchard, growing fruit for the dying industry. The pink of the curtains matched the roses of the carpet. They found pictures of themselves and pondered over them, reminiscing about their clothes and the shape of cars. In his old age her father had become increasingly difficult and her mother had moved into the smaller room, at last free of his bed. It was the room that she and her sister had shared before they left home. Under the heavy sprung bed was her mother's canvas trunk, which had been sent to England in 1950 just before she was born, when she had emigrated south to start her new life. It was stamped with her mother's initials, A.M.N. She pulled it out, its bulky awkwardness frustrating in the lack of space. In the built-in wardrobe hung her father's kilt and accessories. In the corner leaned the cane. She and her sister came across the brown leather case, ripping the leather in their eagerness. No bundles of money. They laughed. Memories were pressed to the back of her mind. She missed not finding the lovely Liberty print clothes that over the years she had made for her mother. She expected them to be there, but they weren't. In their place were off-the-peg, run-of the-mill clothes from mediocre shops. When did that happen? Did she throw them away? Did she give them away? Who was wearing them? It saddened her that they were not in the wardrobe for her to admire and fold and keep. To turn inside out and look at the generous open seams, pressed flat, the raw edges overlocked in matching thread, or as in French seams, totally enclosed. She was possessive about her fine art skill that had allowed her to create beautiful clothes for people. She didn't like the idea of someone else wearing the clothes and not appreciating her expertise and her care and attention to detail, of not understanding the skill involved. Quality was something that she shared with her mother. They would go to the Liberty sale twice a year and drool over the fabrics. She would touch them lightly, holding a corner between her fingers, gently feeling with her thumb or lift a roll from the shelf and hold it up against her mother. They would 'em' and 'ah' leaving the shop with several lengths because they were unable to decide. They would eat in Dickens and Jones from the salad bar and look at their purchases. Glad to sit down. She hoped, when she was gone, her children would find and remember her red coat. Across a crowded shop they could see their mummy, her golden hair streaming over the shoulders of her red coat and find her easily amongst all the other mummies, when they had become scattered or out of sight. They had grown up with the red coat, surely they would remember? Even though he had been dead some years, her father's clothes still hung; the gabardine coat with the poacher's pockets, his Viyella shirts and dusty brogues waiting to be worn. She put the kilt and the case into her mother's trunk, along with the odds and ends, photos, tablecloths, the peg bag that she had made for a Christmas present, the cutlery (which according to her mother's will she would be inheriting) and some bits and bobs for her own children to remind them of their Grandma. Her sister had the blood stained Persian rug, the shirts for her student son and the little wooden cat which rocked.

They did not want her clutter. Each knew that it would just gather dust and eventually be discarded. Neither of them were attached to it any of it; no fond memories, no treasured moments to be reminded of. There was no room for sentiment or a garage full of junk. Age Concern benefited from the ferocious onslaught, as did her mother's neighbours. She felt oddly detached from the frenzy of the day. The waste was terrible; fifty years of hoarding and keeping, crushed and ground at the council tip. There was no time to be nostalgic or emotional. There were no curtains to close, nothing left for burglars to steal. She locked the door, leaving that part of her life behind her.

Examining herself, she took stock. The episode of clearing her mother's house made her realise that she had to keep on top of things while she was fit and able. The third age was approaching rapidly and she didn't want to leave her children finding a congealed pan of fat at the back of her cupboard. Discreetly, she started to dispose of things, nothing obvious. In fact, on the surface you couldn't see the change, but she knew it was there. Her clothes hung freely on the rail and her straw hats were no longer wedged against the ceiling of the wardrobe. The Christmas decorations had a whole shelf to themselves and the National Geographics fitted neatly in a cupboard where the puzzles had been. Things were gradually disappearing, a box of paper patterns recycled, a selection of jigsaw puzzles and games sent off to the charity shop where probably half of them had come from, along with bagfuls of clothes that she had grown tired of. She was pleased. These small changes demonstrated that she was doing something practical about the accumulation of belongings. The problem arose with the things that were not hers. Her children would sneak things into her room and hide them under her bed. There was a bike helmet in its box, numerous school projects, a radio cassette player, soft toys and a plastic space ship. As they had grown up they no longer wanted them in their rooms but did not want them thrown away or given away either. She found herself in a dilemma. She wanted to change and move on but her children, and her husband too, for that matter, wanted things to remain the same, how they had always been. Even though they didn't live with her now, the children would notice if a picture had gone. They would miss an ornament or a wind chime. They would complain to her and say how much they liked such and such and that it had always been there, and make her feel guilty. She didn't feel guilty but at the same time she knew what they meant. They liked the stability, knowing that there had been no change in their absence, nothing moved or thrown away. They questioned change and saw it as uncertainty. It was not surprising that children felt so troubled with a family breakdown if hers were concerned about a picture being removed or the paintwork changed. Would they, like she had done, wonder in thirty years time where the Monopoly went or the pop up wonders of the world book with the unfolding Eiffel Tower went. There was nothing to find under her cushions.

To rid herself of her demons she had always plunged herself into a project and returning from her holiday was no exception. She had hardly unpacked when she launched into DIY, lifting the carpets and removing the doors, allowing herself until Christmas to completely transform the hall, stairs and landing. The ceilings would be pure brilliant white, the walls would be cream and the woodwork would be magnolia, good old safe magnolia, so predictable. Away with the green, the strong garden gate green, first seen on the front of a Good Housekeeping magazine thirty years ago on a wrought iron spiral staircase. It had looked so fresh and sharp against the mainly white room, healthy ferns setting the scene. She had wanted that look in her then small dark hall, the nicotine walls banished for good and a cool airy welcome for friends when they called. The green had not only been applied to the hall but to all the rooms downstairs, doors, frames, skirting boards, pelmets. It had strength and character; it was risky and tended to shock. It had lasted a long time because it had been carefully applied, the bare wood rubbed and primed, and undercoated in grey then the green, chosen from the colour card to match the spiral staircase and mixed in a machine not like the one coat gloss that was now the trend, the quick fix era. The green had long gone in the kitchen and dining room and the hall was its last domain, hanging on defiantly, probably because it was such a mammoth task and the thought of the upheaval, daunting. Her children had not known the colour scheme any other way. They had hung their coats and kicked off their shoes for at least twenty years. They had played under the stairs, jumped down the stairs, climbed into old slippery pink sleeping bags and slipped from the top, giggling and laughing, landing in a heap at the bottom, exhausted. The children liked the green and none of their friends had that colour. They knew that they were home. All the goodbyes and the hellos, the hugs and kisses, going to bed, looking at oneself in the mirror, tapping the barometer, putting the outside light on, finding a pound for the charity envelope; it all happened in the hall. Even when the hall was extended, along with the rest of the house, the green remained. For all its merits, the green had a drawback. Maybe she was being too picky but when the vivid green doors opened onto the murky colours of the Sanderson wallpaper in her bedroom, or the avocado bathroom, it didn't work. For the best effect, the doors were better closed.

No, magnolia was the way forward. The door knobs and hinges were removed and the doors taken away to be stripped of all paint, back to the bare wood, raw and natural. She immersed herself, old track suit bottoms belonging to one of her sons, an old navy tee shirt worn over her own to keep her clean, Radio Four and good sunny mornings. The ceilings were first. Up and down the ladder, her face and hair peppered with speckles of paint. Next was the woodwork. Preparation was everything. She sloughed off the green until it was dull, the grey undercoat reappearing, the wrung out cloth catching on the carpet gripper when she wiped away the fine powdery paint. She vacuumed the underlay and round the skirting boards. She was ready. She levered the lid off the five litre can and dipped her brush into the thick creamy gel, cutting into the smooth glossy surface, on her knees and reaching up, concentrating, carefully concealing the garden gate green for good. The change was immediate. With one stroke of the brush the green had gone. Lastly it was the walls, no rollers for her, she preferred the old comfortable brush that she had used many times before, looked after carefully between each painting session. She didn't let passing comments like "you've missed a bit" or "you can see the brush marks", put her off and there was no room either for sentimental comments. Although progress at times was slow, she was determined and nothing would put her off. The doors were rehung and the carpet refitted well before Christmas. Secretly, she was pleased and the healing process had restored a confidence that the negative thoughts of the summer had eroded.

She kept her mother updated on her progress and promised to show her when the house was back to normal. She liked everything in order and would not have been able to cope with the chaos and change that her house was undergoing. She never saw her lift her head and look around and say "well done" when it was finished. Well, no one said "well done".

Her mother had a fall and broke her leg just above the knee. She was admitted to hospital and stayed for weeks. It was an awful time for her and probably her mother too. Instead of turning left at the roundabout she went straight on and then right two roundabouts later, past the children dangerously crossing the road to the bus stop instead of using the footpath, then left into Standing Way and left again at the hospital then right into the car park. She knew the route with her eyes shut. Then, of course, she needed £2 for the car park. She always had to make sure that she had change to get a parking ticket and after a very busy day these little things really tried her patience. On a couple of occasions she purchased a weekly ticket and placed it on the dashboard when she visited. It allowed her four hours. She walked across the waiting room and up two flights of stairs then along a snaking corridor, past the pictures by local artists, past Mr Henry the vacuum cleaner keeping guard in the corner, ready to "vroom" into action the moment there was a mess. She turned right into the ward. The odious hospital smell greeted her. The smell, was so hard to describe, a mixture of incontinence, reheated food and old age. She had wanted to throw up. The ward was as pleasant as could be, light and cheery for the poor patient in bed, but what about the poor visitors, being subjected to an alien environment, for her it was a daily ordeal, a painful experience. The gloriously warm late summer gave way to more seasonal weather, blustery autumn days, scudding clouds and rain. The dark evenings drew in and the whole place was ablaze with lights.

She would walk into the ward confidently, not a sign of how she felt inside and greeted her mother. She took her hand and kissed her on the cheek. "How are you?" she would say.

"All right," she would reply.

"What did you have for your lunch?" she would say.

"Salad," she would reply.

She hadn't had salad. She lied or it had slipped her mind completely that she had had any lunch at all. She would tell her about her day and what she was cooking for supper. Suitable topics were soon exhausted. It was hard going. It was as though her mother had forgotten how to speak. She didn't make conversation, she just stared around the ward taking in the shapes and the people as though they were from another planet She praised and encouraged as if she were a child, without success. Sometimes she dozed. She didn't want the TV, she didn't want a newspaper or a magazine or a book. She didn't want anything. On a good day she managed to stay half an hour. She busied herself in her locker, sorting her shitty washing, arranging things on her table, plumping her pillows, helping her with her tea, persuading her to eat. She always visited on her own. No one offered to go with her and she didn't ask anyone. She already knew how they would respond. It was a thankless job and she wondered if her mother would notice if she didn't go, but she felt compelled to go; the guilt of not going would have been too great. Emotions ran high, trying to please and comfort and console. Why did she feel so hopelessly inadequate, so useless, so drained? Some people cared for their loved ones for years without complaining, putting them first, and this in itself made her feel that she was not trying.

She should have been rebellious, stood her ground, put her foot down right from the start and said that she would visit twice a week, once at the weekend and once during the week. That is what her sister would have done. She would not have let anyone or anything determine or rule her day. Even when she was young and sent to her room when she wanted to be out, she would wait until the coast was clear and climb out of her bedroom window and shin down the drainpipe. She would do what she wanted. She was not like her sister. She conformed and did as she was told and always had done. Her mother expected her to go, and obediently, she did. There was no need to say anything. She would kiss her mother goodbye and make her way back to her car, taking a deep breath before the smoky fog at the main entrance. That entrance was a health risk, so desperate were patients to have a cigarette that they would walk or get pushed in a wheelchair still attached to their dextrose drips and incontinence drains, hovering at the entrance, shivering with cold, polluting the air. The banner across the front door promoted a smoke free hospital in the New Year. Not before time.

She had a phone call. Her mother was going home. Brilliant, but for whom? There was no need to get excited. She was hardly at home a week when she slipped off her chair and broke her hip. She was back in hospital. This was not good news, and although she was comfortable she was becoming institutionalised, becoming more and more dependent on other people. She had lost her fight and her will and her muscles. Sometimes her mother became unwell and didn't know who she was. It all seemed so wretchedly pointless. She couldn't look at her. She did not seem to be her mother as she had known her. Sometimes, she caught her looking at her in a secretive sort of way, her mouth sunken, her thin smile wavy and closed over her gums or she would look surprised, as though she hadn't seen her for years, like a long lost friend. Or she would look frightened and anxious, suffering like a fox caught in a trap. It was awful. The daily wearing down, the burden of it all could go on indefinitely. She felt resentful and angry, angry that she could do no more and what she was doing simply wasn't enough. If she had had someone to share her frustration and despair it might have helped. People enquired about her mother's progress. Her husband asked how mum was. Her sister phoned every few days to see how the patient was but no one asked how she was, if she was coping. Of course, if anyone did, she always assured them that she was fine, which was not entirely true. Hope was restored a little when the lady on the desk where she bought her weekly parking ticket, kindly asked if she was eating properly and getting enough sleep. At the time she thought how nice it was that this perfect stranger had shown sympathy and genuine concern for her. She felt comforted as she walked across the waiting room, up the two flights of stairs, along the snaking corridor and into the ward. It was not too much to ask. It was hardly out of her way. Next year she might not be there to visit, then how would she feel? Thankfully her mother regained her strength enough to return home in January. She did not go back to the hospital.

As usual, she was getting ready to face the world. It was just after seven and she always allowed herself half an hour for the procedure, showering, brushing the hair and the teeth, fixing the face, dressing, attaching the earrings and spraying some perfume. Voila! The phone rang and she knew. Half dressed she ran downstairs and lifted the receiver and she knew. The harrowing event of dying was over. Heather led the way, chatting as she did so, along the familiar blue carpeted landing to her mother's room. Less than twelve hours earlier she had been sitting beside her mother, holding her hand, looking at her, watching for the gentle rise and fall of her duvet and when it didn't move, listening for her quiet shallow breathing. She remembered watching her babies asleep, mesmerized by the gentle rise and fall of their cot covers, listening, almost paranoid when the covers stopped moving. Her mother hadn't really said anything, just briefly opened her eyes and half smiled at her daughter. The curtains were still drawn tightly, as her mother liked them, not a splinter of sunlight fell across the room and the ceiling light was on. The room was how it had been the evening before, a box of After Eights, unopened on the side, her glasses with the chain wrapped around, her new blue slippers that she had been so delighted with beside the bed. She had felt sorry for her mother, struggling with old age, becoming increasingly dependent on others, frustrated. Now she lay under her duvet as though asleep, her mouth closed in a thin wavy line her face calm and relaxed, at peace. 'There's no more pain, there's no more sorrow. They've all gone, gone in the years babe.' After a few moments reality dawned. Her mother was dead and she felt overwhelmed with the burden of it all. She needed to feel normal. She thanked Heather and hastily said goodbye. Stepping out into the fresh April air she walked blindly to the car. The cat arched its back and stretched. Her mother was not normally fond of cats but liked to stroke Cat when they sat outside on golden summer days. Cat liked the attention and basked warm and heavy, purring deeply, the tip of his tail just lightly twitching. It was an outdoor cat and never ventured inside. Even in the winter when she visited her mother Cat would curl up on the bonnet of the car, the warmth of the engine comforting. She would recite:

The Owl and the Pussy cat went to sea
In a beautiful pea-green boat.
They took some honey and plenty of money,
Wrapped up in a five pound note.
The Owl looked up to the stars above,
And sang to a small guitar,
"O lovely Pussy! O Pussy, my love,
What a beautiful Pussy you are,
You are!
What a beautiful Pussy you are!"
Pussy said to the Owl, " You elegant fowl!
How charmingly sweet you sing!
O let us be married! Too long we have tarried:
But what shall we do for a ring?"
They sailed away for a year and a day,
To the land where the Bong tree grows,
And there in a wood a Piggy-wig stood,
With a ring at the end of his nose,
His nose,
With a ring at the end of his nose.
"Dear Pig, are you willing to sell for one shilling
Your ring?" Said the Piggy, "I will."
So they took it away, and were married next day
By the Turkey who lives on the hill.
They dined on mince and slices of quince,
Which they ate with a runcible spoon;
And hand in hand, on the edge of the sand,
They danced by the light of the moon.

They met at The Farm Inn and she pushed the 'What is it all about?' thoughts to the back of her mind when she saw her children and her sister's children. They looked amazing, smartly dressed in dark shirts and suits, tall, strong, healthy, intelligent, the whole world before them. They looked wonderful, fresh, funny, sensitive, unsure, sociable and she thought, this is what it is all about. Her mother would have been so proud of her grandchildren. It was such a good moment.

Dust danced in the shaft of sunlight that fell over the coffin. Inside the oak veneer, her mother's choice, her mother lay in a pink shroud, her choice. She trusted that she was at last at rest. She had declined the offer of viewing the body and took upon herself the decision that no one would want to view. It was difficult enough to get her family to visit her mother when she was alive, it was unlikely they would want to see her dead. She thought that it must be difficult to decide what to wear on your funeral day years in advance of the event. After all, no one would see you. She imagined the pink shroud looking like the bri-nylon sheets her mother used to have, shocks of static lighting up, then dripping and melting when the fire consumed, moulding round her, vacuumed like a pack of bacon. It was strange, knowing that she was just there inside the coffin, just a few feet from her. She stood next to her husband in the front pew, opposite the lectern. The readings had been chosen with great care but the hymns which were rousing and favourites of her mother's and hers too, were impossible to sing; notes came out distorted or not at all. Her mother had been scared of dying, scared of the transition from earth to heaven, scared of being naked and exposed, vulnerable. But she need not have been; it was such an occasion. In contrast with the Tesco mince pies she had provided at her Father's funeral she launched into making rounds of shortbread, just like her mother's, layered between sheets of greaseproof paper. Her mother's shortbread had such a hallmark. Her sister had potted up cuckoo pint and primroses in terracotta pots, and gathered bluebells. The previous evening she had picked cowslips from her friend's arboretum and placed them in her Minton teapot. It was a glorious spring day, a day to be living and in the minds of her family and friends, her mother was very much alive. Leaning against a pew, her cousin said to her that they were the old ones now. She had never thought of herself as old. She didn't feel old, she felt full of energy, full of vim.

***

A week later, hanging on the rail in the hospice shop were her mother's trousers, she knew that they were her mother's because she could see where her nametape had been unpicked and the remains of the thread were still embedded in the waistband. Her mother had taken to wearing trousers in her old age. Her daughter had taken her in the wheelchair to Marks and Spencers and she had chosen a pair and tried them on. She stood up precariously and was pleased with her reflection, smart and comfortable, a sought-after combination. Her mother said that when she was young she had worn trousers, but her brother made hurtful comments about her appearance and she had never worn them since. They hung on a green plastic hanger. Slowly, she brushed her hand over the fabric. She went back a week later. They had gone.

She took to drinking. Bottles and bottles of wine were consumed. There was always a bottle in the cupboard, ready to pour or in the fridge, chilling. It didn't matter, red or white. Ice cold Carling or Carlsberg, never without. She was never drunk, just energetic, restless, numb. Of course being the year of the World Cup didn't help. Offers in Tesco were good, too good to miss. She learnt to place the twenty four pack with the bar code up for easy swiping and collected a great many wine carriers. The euphoria ended along with the razzamatazz of the World Cup.

She liked a drink; it soothed and lubricated. It gave her a confidence, a self assurance that she otherwise lacked. Alcohol oiled and greased her normally stunted conversations and words tripped off her tongue. She used interesting words, not usually part of her vocabulary. She became impulsive and her inhibitions forgotten. The thought of a glass of wine conjured up an image, a sociable image, relaxed and informal, one of affluence and success. Drinking wine was a comparatively recent indulgence, once the domain of the wealthy but now enjoyed by the masses at any time, not just the bottle of Sauterne with the Christmas lunch. Now wines were flown in from all around the world to satisfy an insatiable lust, a craving for oblivion, to blur out the working week and make it all seem manageable. Reaching for a bottle of wine was not a difficult decision. It was either red or white or both. If it was red she knew that it was all hers. If it was white then it would be shared with her husband. Sometimes she disguised it in sangria, or mulled, spiced and medicinal on a cold winter's day. She usually chose European. Even though they were cheaper, she didn't go for South African or South American because morally it didn't seem right. She had visions of the workers being exploited. Nor did she go for Californian wines, that didn't seem right either, the western states did not need subsidising, also there was the fact that it had to travel so far. Then how did she explain Australian wines which she found fruity and spicy, ideal with pasta and meat dishes? Well it was the pink bit on the map so that made it all right. The good deals were hard to resist. If it was a white wine she would snuggle the frozen peas around it in the carrier bag to start the chilling process, then into the fridge. Red wine would sit on the table, teasing and tempting waiting for the moment. She had an assortment of glasses. Her latest ones were cheap, fifty pence each but they were big and generous. Half a bottle per glass, no need to sip cautiously. She would remove the tamperproof seal, and depending on whither it was plastic or foil, it would ease off without a problem or she would be madly cutting through it with a knife. Eagerly, she would search the drawer for the corkscrew, (which inevitably had found its way to the bottom of the drawer) twisting the thread into the cork and levering the handles, forcing them down to release with a soft kiss. Then pouring, the anticipation increasing, she would nearly fill the glass, swallowing the fruity red water, savouring its warmth, smelling the sun and the soil. The new screw topped wines were a godsend and speeded up the process but somehow they did not seem that they would be so alcoholic, more like a non-alcoholic wine. How can that be called wine? Of course the ritual of removing the cork was part of the performance, the crescendo in that soft kiss and the finale, tasting and swallowing, letting it consume and pulse through her body, numbing, depriving, yet intensifying sensation. Plastic corks were to her a cheap idea and could not possibly compete with cork, they were just as bad as a screw top. It was just as well that she did not keep a stock of alcohol in the house. Purchases were on the spur, bought and consumed there and then, within hours. She liked the heady feeling of not being quite in control just as much as she liked the feeling of being in control. Without control and order she was thrown into disarray and chaos. In the morning she would wake parched and dry, her throat like sandpaper needing endless cups of tea to restore the balance, vowing not to drink again. It was short lived. She did not trust herself.

In her mother's kitchen cupboard she remembered finding several bottles of Harvey's Bristol Cream. Some were unopened and some had been partly consumed. She had seen her mother use it liberally in soups and gravies but twelve bottles was a lot to account for. Anyway, her mother no longer cooked. Her mother was drinking, drinking to blot out her existence. She did not trust her mother either.

Her loss was hard to define. Now that her mother was no longer there she felt dispensed with, she was no longer useful and necessary. After fifty-five years she was no

115

longer worth anything to her mother, no longer loved by her and that special bond which had endured and held fast for all that time had gone. Being valued was important to her. It made her feel good. She felt that she was paying attention to the things that mattered. Of course, there were frustrations and she knew that her mother's caustic tongue hurt. When she came for lunch one day she made the saucy chocolate pudding, a favourite with everyone. "I've tasted better." The grandchildren were aghast. How could anyone say that to their mummy? She was blunt and often rude. Her mother's pinched drawn expression was enough to kill. But that was her getting old and anxious and however many times her daughter said that there was no need to worry, it made no difference. She did not miss her mother's demands. She expected her daughter to do things at the drop of a hat, collect her skirt from the dry cleaner's or magically produce wool to darn her jumper and she never understood that she went to work from seven-thirty until five-thirty and could only run errands on Saturdays. If she hadn't brought her biscuits to feed the squirrels, she scavenged around the residents at elevenses or afternoon tea complaining that her daughter hadn't brought any biscuits. Occasionally, she had to speak to her mother about her behaviour and lack of manners, such a long way from the real her. Her daughter had to be firm and would raise her voice, partly so her mother would hear her and partly to tell her off. Her mother would retaliate and she would answer back sharply. Exhausted they would fall silent.

Her son was small and snuggled, foetal position, in the bottom of a paper carrier bag, one of those smart save the planet bags with a tightly rolled paper handle. She had collected him from a local nursery in a not very desirable area. She strapped the seat belt over the bag but could see in the rear view mirror as she was driving that it had become unsteady and needed repositioning. As she pulled over onto the grass verge she noticed a dog curled up in the hedgerow. She turned off the engine and released her seat belt, opened the door and got out of the car. She moved her seat forward in order to reach her son. The dog was interested and stood up. It was the same dog as on Tutankhamen's golden chariot and once unfolded stood much higher than the car, long, long legs and a long thin rough haired body and it was cowering down trying to get at her son, sniffing in the carrier bag. Beside her, her husband was saying "It's all right, it's all right, it's all right."

She loved being submerged, the weightlessness, the ease of movement, the effortless stretching out her curved shape and although her technique was not textbook, it was acceptable, like holding knives and forks or a pen, so many variations, each workable. She remembered filling the bathroom sink with cold water right up to the overflow then taking a deep breath and slowly submerging her face holding her breath for as long as possible, counting and daring herself to open her eyes, looking at the black rubber plug seeing a million tiny bubbles clinging to its chain, hearing the water drain into murky green overflow, running out of breath and resurfacing. She would pat her face dry and refill the sink for another go.

She didn't like the water in her eyes. When her goggles felt too tight she would release the pressure and wear them on her forehead. Forgetting, she would swim below the surface. Immediately her eyes were aggravated and she would stop and rub them, then reposition the goggles over the dented skin around her eyes. At the pool she saw babies and slippery children fearless, their eyes open, bobbing about as though it was the most natural thing in the world.

"Excuse me, Senorita. Esta libre la tumbona?" She was surprised that anyone at the pool should speak to her and put her arm up to block out the harsh white light in order to see the man who was speaking. No she replied and gestured to the Senor to take it. Why was there not a polite way of addressing people at home, instead of the awkward hesitant, hovering indecision. She had come across the lido when left to her own devices. Her husband had gone

fishing and she decided to explore the town, systematically walking around the outskirts working her way along the narrow streets backwards and forwards so that she missed nothing. She was soon hot and tired. Mad dogs. She was drawn to the laughter and splashing before she saw it. At last, there was something in the isolated hilltop town for her. She peered through the fence. There were two pools, a paddling pool set in a grassy area under the trees, children and toddlers playing and having fun, and a swimming pool. This was where the locals were, and who could blame them? Being submerged was the only place to be in the soaring temperatures. The sun beat down on the concrete slabs. They were red hot and she needed to leap in one jump from the sun chair to the water to avoid burnt soles. Pools were fine but didn't compare to the sea. For her the sea was exhilarating and exciting. She never tired of its constant motion, it was reliable, the unrelenting forward and back, forward and back, regular, like a beating heart, always the same, yet depending on the weather, always changing, waves churning and building, rolling and breaking smoothing out footprints, leaving a tide line fringed with foam. She liked the sound that the sea made, the wash on the pebbles, the roar and pounding on rocks, salty spume thrown against the cliffs, the gentle lap on hard sand. Waves whipped up in the wind, the salty taste in the air, white horses far out to sea, glinting in sunlight. Even in the winter, wrapped against the cold, being by the sea heightened her senses, put everything in perspective. She never wanted to leave the beach until the very end of the day. In this she was childlike, even now, a grown up, she would stay until the sun had set and the crowds had gone home. She knew it was time to go when the beach boys collected and stacked the sun chairs and closed the parasols but she would sit on the trampled sand, sitting as close as she dare to the waves quietly breaking on the shore. The fluttering flags had ceased and apart from a dog running about, the beach was all hers:

***

"I must go down to the seas again, to the lonely sea and the sky,

And all I ask is a tall ship and a star to steer her by;

And the wheel's kick and the wind's song and the white sails shaking,

And the grey mist on the sea's face, and a grey dawn breaking.

I must go down to the seas again, for the call of the running tide

Is a wild call and a clear call that may not be denied;

And all I ask is a windy day with the white clouds flying,

And the flung spray and the blown spume, and the sea gulls crying.

I must go down to the seas again, to the vagrant gypsy life,

To the gull's way and the whale's way, where the wind's like a whetted knife;

And all I ask is a merry yarn from a laughing fellow rover,

And a quiet sleep and a sweet dream when the long trick's over.

Swimming soothed and calmed She liked the fact that when she was swimming she couldn't do anything else. She might smile or acknowledge someone she knew but apart from that she concentrated fully. It was just about the only thing that she did purely for herself. She liked the smooth pearly feel on her skin. She liked the movement of the water against her body, the swirling and rolling, especially the sea, catching a wave, buoyant, being lifted and carried like a

119

piece of driftwood. The pool was different, but the feeling of movement was still there, swishing and swirling, spiralling, swallowing her up in a vortex, rolling her around below the surface, water unfurling around her like a roll of silk, slipping and clinging then ballooning out, a million bubbles bursting then flat calm, like a mill pond, waiting for the wash of the wave. She liked seeing the pool still; so still that she could see the sky and the shapes of the clouds mirrored and reflected in the water.

She never ceased to marvel when she paddled in the shallows and looked out to the horizon. It was like being on the edge of the world and if you travelled across the sea from Morocco the next country would be Mexico – the same unremitting sea that Columbus had sailed across in the 15th century when he discovered America. The Mediterranean Sea was the same; the peoples of the ancient world, the Greeks, the Romans and the Egyptians all travelling and trading in their wooden boats. In her mind she pictured how it might have been hundreds and thousands of years ago. Maybe on holiday, because she had time to indulge in the luxury of thinking, she formed a romantic impression of the past, but knew too that there must have been hideous scenes, starvation, rats, men drowning, cruelty but that was all part of the lure like the sirens calling sailors to their death. Mythology, bible stories, fairy tales and legends came alive in her mind. When the instructor said that they would dive off the Sinai desert her mind rushed back to when she was a Sunday school teacher, barely fifteen, when she scanned her old bible regularly for stories and remembered Moses and the ten commandments on Mount Sinai: "The Lord said unto Moses, Ye have seen that I have talked with you from heaven." She thought that it was amazing that she should be there seeing the Sinai desert from the dive boat. Through the shimmering haze caused by the blistering heat she pictured Moses wearing his djellaba treading over the rough stony ground, his arms stretched out. A mirage. She could see nothing except miles and miles of ochre coloured rocks. Nothing lived, not a blade of green. She reached for her bibles from the bookcase. One had been given by a man called John Phillips whom her mother had enlisted to help her daughter with her school work. She found her old red bible in the book case, its cotton binding fraying. She turned the thin faded pages to the pale delicate maps of the ancient world, Mesopotamia, Assyria, Persia, Asia Minor, Arabia, Samaria, Judea, old names but still troubled and war-torn.

Quinquireime of Nineveh from distant Ophir

Rowing home to haven in sunny Palestine.

With a cargo of ivory

And apes and peacocks

Sandlewood and cedarwood and sweet white wine.

Stately Spanish galleon coming from the Isthmus

Dipping through the tropics by the palm green shores.

With a cargo of diamonds

Emeralds, amethysts

Topazes and cinnamon and gold moidores.

Dirty British coaster with a salt-caked smoke stack.

Butting through the channel in the mad March days.

With a cargo of Tyne coal

Road-rail, pig lead,

Firewood, iron wear and cheap tin trays.

The soft, muted colours of the illustrations depicted scenes from the bible; low mud brick houses open to the sky, which she called the Bethlehem houses, donkeys laden, desolate waste areas, the arid, parched dryness. She had seen it. It really was like that. For her the desert held a fascination; its vastness, its remoteness, its isolation, its extreme climate. Of course, the Bethlehem houses had aerials and satellite dishes and spoilt the skyline and her illusion. Tareq, the guide on a visit to Luxor, assured her that the local people had all the mod cons and twentieth century lifestyle. At times she was not convinced. The land below the sea was just as exciting as the land above, never seen before. She could never have contemplated what it would be like, or what it stirred in her. Standing on the land but below the sea, filled her with wonder. It was awesome. No words could describe her feelings as she stood on the sandy sea bed. On her left the land just fell away, dropping into the never-ending bowels of the earth, the deep black abyss. She signalled the universal OK sign with her thumb and index finger to her buddy. It didn't matter where or when, she always went on a big adventure in her mind.

After church, on Ascension Day, the children at her junior school were always taken on a school trip. For her, it was a special event. Altogether, she went on three trips and each held a special place in her mind and even now, fifty years later each is vividly recollected. The days were carefully structured and always included a river cruise from Westminster Pier. The children formed a single line and went on board, sitting on the varnished wooden seats in neat rows. She loved the river, the old derelict warehouses on the Thames, the winches silhouetted like gallows, the old docks, men lifting and hoisting. She remembered the Tower of London, when she imagined herself being taken to Traitors' Gate in a small rowing boat and having to wait for low tide, the black water lapping against the outer wall of the Tower, hushed voices, the portcullis creaking as it was lifting and being thrown in a dark, damp dungeon, cold and frightened, waiting to be beheaded. She remembered disembarking from the pleasure cruiser at Hampton Court and seeing Henry VIII's Palace and the Great Hall where he would have had banquets and sat at the great long table swilling wine out of goblets and throwing bones over his shoulder for his dogs to find, and jesters in red and yellow harlequin tunic and tights and musicians playing the lute and the narrow bunks on the Cutty Sark. The clippers were small. From pictures she had imagined them bigger but they were adventurous and brave and brought back new and exciting foods to England. She didn't agree with all the modern audio-visual techniques that were now in place in castles and museums. To her, the keepers of these places were removing the authenticity. She had seen it how it really was, lit only by a 40 watt bulb. These places came alive in her mind and even now a favourite activity was to take a boat trip along the Thames. She must find time to see the Thames barrier. But it didn't matter where it was, old textile mills in Derby, prosperous in their day, now redundant, broken panes, brickwork loose, graffiti, rose bay willow herb softening the edges, seeds blown and scattered across the wasteland, a dumping ground for mattresses, a short cut to somewhere else. She would peer inside, the monumental arcs of steel supporting, standing proud, defiant, strong, their innards gouged out, machines silenced and voices mute.

She sat on the train, just looking, staring out at the countryside. She turned her head and saw the familiar church on the hill, which had overlooked her life, as it did in the painting (left to her by her mother), that now hung above the stair well. Beyond that, the church where she had got married on that cool February afternoon, nestling in the chestnut trees, their buds sticky, waiting to burst. There was always a nature table at school. Children would be encouraged to bring in seasonal offerings and arrange them for the class to see. She remembered taking pussy willows and hazel catkins at this time of year and arranging them in a jam jar. In the autumn she would take hips and haws and golden leaves, pressed flat between sheets of newspaper. Behind the church were the Knolls, a wild overgrown area where she and her husband used to walk as lovers. Fluttering harebells and bee orchids clung to the hoe in the shallow chalky soil. She saw the lion etched into the Downs. She first went to the zoo in 1959, the hot busy summer. A day off school had been authorised because her relations, who were visiting from Scotland, were taking her. The main purpose of their visit was to be her godparents, because although she was eight, the occasion had not been marked. The trip to the zoo was such a special treat and one not afforded by her parents. Besides seeing all the animals she also went to the restaurant, which overlooked the flamingos, and had ham salad. At the end she was allowed to choose a small gift and a postcard from the shop. It was surely the best day of her life.

She tried to remember her sister and realised that she couldn't. Oh, she could look at photographs and remember her, but she couldn't actually remember her as a person, not as a child, not as a sister, not as a friend. She vaguely remembered playing hospitals and schools in the bedroom that they shared. They would arrange the dolls and teddies in rows on the floor. One or two were naughty and fell over. She and her sister would teach them to read and prop a book on their laps and do sums on the blackboard. If they were ill, she and her sister would put on their nurses' aprons that had a red cross on the bib and pretend to take their temperatures and listen to their chests with the plastic stethoscope and make them better by giving them pretend medicine which was really water from the bathroom tap. She remembered playing in the shed, not that there was much room, it was full of rubbish, pieces of wood, old paint cans; they would sort it all out, clearing a space to play. Butterflies, papery thin pressed into the corners of the unreachable window, their wings closed, dry and brittle, their energetic flapping to escape, long ceased. Spiders had joined in, weaving a web of fabric around them enclosing them forever. Her sister had a pony called Domino and she spent all her time cleaning the tack and brushing him down, talking to her horsy friends. Of course she was envious. Her sister passed her 11 plus and went to a different school. She wore a grey felt hat. She played the recorder. She didn't have a recorder, she never learnt to play Frere Jacque. When she was older she used to hurt her mother's feelings by refusing to eat her mother's meals, preferring to make a Vesta chicken chow mein, out of a packet followed by chocolate instant whip. Also, she smoked cigarettes. Her mother vented displeasure and confided in her. "She's just like your father." She simply did not remember her.

The trestle decorating tables were set out precariously across the grassy slope overlooking the village. The bras were neatly folded inside each other and displayed according to the cup size. The assistants around her spoke French and wore black knee length skirts and white blouses. Some designs depicted religious scenes from stained glass windows and the French Revolution. The detail was exquisite and the fabrics finely moulded in stretch lace to uplift and accentuate the curve.

The shallow sun lit up the trees and everywhere was bathed in a mysterious golden glow. She felt uninvited, as though she was intruding into a private place. All around petals of gold fluttered and spiralled, lightly resting, overlapping and interlacing to form a woven carpet beneath the trees. Shadows, long and distorted, lay across the road, flat and black stopping suddenly at kerbs and walls to rise abruptly without support. Leaves, rubbing along, leaping and laughing on their way to the gutter, crisp and curled, rolling, delirious, free to blow about and be themselves. She pushed her gloved hand through her husband's crooked elbow. They walked like this during the winter in order to keep each other warm. It was clear and cool, a late afternoon in early December. She remembered just such Saturday afternoons nearly fifty years ago when she and other Sunday school members used to go to Christine's house at the top of the hill and make gifts for the forthcoming Christmas bazaar. She used to dress a wooden spoon with a duster and a dish mop and make milk jug covers out of muslin, weighted down with coloured beads and make needlework cases out of felt and calendars out of old birthday cards and satin ribbons.

The train pulled into Euston station, efficient and on time. Platform fifteen, the last platform. No staff to greet, no machines to snatch your ticket, read it then snap it out. It was cold and she walked briskly. At the entrance to the station stood a young Asian man, hands in his pockets. He anxiously searched the crowd, looking. Catching her eye, he found her. His face broke into a smile, his dark eyes danced, transfixed. She had seen the girl on the train, smooth skinned and stunning. They kissed and hugged and kissed again, oblivious to the swarm of people streaming past them. They linked arms, pressing against each other, moving and kissing, absorbed. He took her carrier bag and they disappeared as one into the underground.

On the very same platform she remembered feeling like that, consumed by an intense melting feeling, the fiery knot in the pit of her stomach, catching his warm brown eyes scanning the people spilling from the train, quickening her pace, warmth dissolving over his face, their smiles broadening, their deep passionate kiss, unaware of every day life around them. His arms enfolded, holding her close, squeezing her tight. A misty fusion fell over them. He was there, dependable and reliable as he still was.

When she eleven and went to the secondary modern she saw him for the first time. He was as dark as she was fair. He was tall and his hair fell over his forehead. His blazer hung loose on his lean coat hanger shape. From a distance she idolised him. If she saw him in the corridor or lined up waiting to go into the science labs, her heart literally skipped a beat. He was good at sport and had a strong desire to win. At lunchtimes she would sit dreamily on the raised bank near the tennis courts and watch him thrash his opponent, her mind a romantic fog. Needless to say, it was difficult to concentrate in the afternoons. To her, he was different. He had a foreign sounding name and that intrigued. His strong physical attraction was always on her mind. She wasn't sure if it was love at first sight because she wasn't entirely sure what love was. She wasn't confident. She had freckles and auburn hair and skin to match. She wasn't fashionable or cool. She was quiet and timid, shy with nothing much to say. She went unnoticed for years. Then out of the blue, she went to his house, She had become friendly with his sister. By then he had left school to be an apprentice and must have come home for lunch. He said "hello" and that was it, he fell in love with her. Her love for him had never gone away.

Preoccupied, playing football and cricket and going fishing, his passion in life, there had been little time to notice her. It wasn't that he didn't notice girls; in fact, he had a crush on her friend Pauline. There was a rumour about her smooth silky knickers and he fantasised, along with others, about her tight little arse and the intoxicating flesh at the top of her stockings. She wanted him to lust after her like that but knew that wouldn't happen; no she was different. She was different all right. He was not one to make the first move. He just couldn't be asked, which didn't fill her with confidence. She kissed him in his parents' front room, the room kept for best in case visitors called. It was a cold room and sparsely furnished. A wine-coloured three seater settee and two armchairs faced the fireplace. In the depths of winter a two barred electric fire heated the room. The room overlooked the main road and the traffic could be heard plainly through the thin Victorian glass. Afterwards she felt that she had been hasty. He might have thought her forward and been put off. He liked her; she had a nice face and a nice voice, she wasn't demanding on his time and she introduced him to girly activities like going out and doing things. She had romantic ideas and he went along with them, seduced by her eagerness. The months rolled into years.

***

She didn't imagine that he had been infatuated by her and in a way she was relieved that he hadn't. She knew that men were always leering at girls and commenting upon the way they looked, the size of their tits or the shape of their legs. She was so conscious of what she wore and how she wore it so as not to draw attention to herself. Compared to many, she might have seemed sensible and practical, plain. She avoided anything that made her look cheap or promiscuous. The awful thing was that she did feel like that, her childhood years, damaged, and her teenage years racked with guilt. He didn't pore over her, it wasn't his style. He was quietly caring and protective. Always there, he never questioned. She didn't like men; she only knew a few and tended to tar them all with the same brush. Her aggressive father, his rough Irish friends, the man next door who managed to get her signed photographs of the latest bands, the boy she called Wayne who worked for the council painting the council houses; called Wayne because he looked like Wayne Fontana. She never knew his real name because she didn't actually speak to him. Why did so many men think that they were superior? Why did they belittle and bully? Couldn't the maths teacher see that she didn't get it and struggled for the answer when he called her name? She felt humiliated. Deep within, a wave of heat erupted, flooding towards her face, blood vessels distended, heightening her colouring. Tongue tied, sheer panic set in, everyone turned to look. Why did her partner have to be the village idiot, chosen for her by her teacher in country dancing lessons? Why couldn't it be Tony or Keith, who were nice looking boys? Life was already mapped out. When she was older, there was Michael, who lived with his fireman friend, which in her naivety she didn't understand. She sometimes sat next to him on the bus on the way to college and they just chatted. Then there was Gavin, her tutor who was tall and willowy. Her mother would have said he was effeminate; she didn't understand that either. To her they were different but they asked nothing of her and she liked them for that. Where there was scaffolding there were wolf whistles and flying comments thrown from a great height. To those throwing them it was a laugh, just part of their day but to her it was torture, she would scuttle past, cowering. She knew men spoke like that, vulgar and coarse. Her father for one, who never missed an opportunity to hurl abuse: " You fucking bastard."

During the fifties and even beyond that she could remember bras being made of cotton, by stitching bands of material together to form two cones. It was not a natural shape. She could remember a teacher who was young and fashionable in her tight pencil slim skirts and fine jumpers pulled up at the elbow ready for business. Anyone could see, including her father that she wore that type of bra. He would lust after her high tits and her tight arse. No one was exempt; big girls were called heavy rollers and big girls in trousers, still quite unusual then, were called elephant arse. She was out of her depth in the local milk bar, the glares and stares, perched on a tall chrome stool looking through the glass wall onto the passers by, trying to be smart and cool. She wasn't in the least sophisticated; no, that was the trouble. A tea room would have been more in keeping with how she felt. She even went to the school dance in her Start-rite shoes. Her self esteem was never good; she criticised herself. In an effort to smooth her dimpled legs she would smother them in cream and wrap them in carrier bags before going to bed. Looking at photos now she could see that she wasn't fat or overweight but at the time of the mini skirt and hot pants, long, smooth, flawless legs were essential. Hers had none of those qualities. Growing up seemed a constant challenge; almost life-threatening.

Scum had collected and was floating on the surface. The hard water gnawed at her skin, making it feel dry and damaged. She turned off the tap and leaned back. The bath, gull grey where the relentless dripping tap had stained, still dripping now as it had done for years. There was no splash just a perfect ripple where the drips disturbed the surface. The bristles of her big plastic rollers dug in and hurt her scalp. She closed her eyes, drowning in sorrow. Was she doing the right thing? Was it right to marry the man who loved her so dearly and not be honest with him. It tormented her as it had done for years. But now it was crunch time, no going back, a lasting binding contract. It seemed to her that she was deceiving him and fooling her friends. To her this seemed to be worse than the original crime. She was responsible for all the pain that coursed through her; it was all her fault. She felt dishonest and knew that she was living a lie. It was never right that she should be walking down the aisle on her father's arm, everyone turning to look when the organ started to play the wedding march. Everyone would be nice to him, flattering and congratulating him. Her father would enjoy the attention, smiling and showing his smooth gold tooth. Yet he knew, he knew all along about his wife and his eight children and his second family and the fact that he wasn't divorced but co-habited with her mother. Although no one knew at the time of her awful childhood experiences, her special day was spoilt, marred and tarnished. She would like to have got married secretly but how could she have explained why? She might have lost the one person who meant more to her than anything. She pulled out the plug, letting her grief drain away. The scum clung to the bath. She lingered over her face, carefully arranged her hair and fastened the many covered buttons on her warm Liberty print dress. It was not a traditional white wedding. It was more informal and held quite late in the afternoon. Through her thick platform soles she did not feel the rough uneven path of life that led towards the church. Feathers of light, miles high, stippled the cold blue February sky.

Ten years after first setting eyes on him, she married the man of her childhood dreams and cast insane thoughts of telling any one of her family secrets to the back of her mind. Sometimes she thought that she would never be free.

Her husband ached for a son. She knew that the honeymoon period was over and after five years, the painful memories were about to resurface. She went to her G.P. with some minor ailment and came out an hour later awash with tears. Confiding in him had been harrowing. He had leaned back in his chair contemplating what she had said. She had felt as though she was on trial, having to give evidence and explain such personal details. Some words took ages to come out, some just didn't come out at all. There were long silences and intermittent sobs. He watched her, he fiddled with his pen, his elbows resting on the arms of his swivel chair. Clearly he was finding it difficult. There was nothing he could prescribe to fix her festering life and advised her to speak to her husband. Meekly, she nodded, knowing that she couldn't.

It wasn't long before she felt oddly strange, nauseous, quite frankly, wretched. After that she bloomed, her flat stomach stretched to the size of a watermelon, hard and ripe. Her belly button turned itself inside out, like the end of a balloon. As space became limited his elbows and feet kicked out agitated, as she felt in tucked in sheets. She would encourage her husband to feel the ripening melon and feel him through her skin. They had always called the melon a he but it was confirmed by Mr Shar in the furnishing department in John Lewis's Oxford Street store. She and her husband had been to the Chelsea Flower Show and afterwards had called in to get curtain fabric for their recently decorated bedroom. Mr Shar unrolled the bolt of cloth. She was aware of him watching her. "It will be a boy," he said. " I can tell," he continued, measuring out the smoky pink fabric.

"I have never been wrong in my predictions." He was pleased and smiling; he folded the material and took a carrier bag from beneath the counter.

"It will be a boy," he assured as he handed her husband the bag. Her whole body flourished. She would

131

look at herself in the bath, rampant and fleshy, voluptuous, her breasts full and heavy, resting on her expanding stomach. Unlike today, when pregnancy is almost a fashion statement, she loved hiding her body under a big dress, no passing comments, no wolf whistles. She thought that her mother would share her emotions, her fear and excitement and offer advice, but she didn't.

With one final push, he slithered out on to the disposable mat between her legs, all sticky and bloody. She was elated. Truly she had done it, survived all the gloved hands prodding and feeling, survived the hard white lights looking, searching her soul. There would be more babies. She was euphoric. True enough, subsequent babies followed, each surrounded with her precious love. She could remember the exact moment of knowing that her last baby was safely embedded in her womb. She had been sewing on her machine in the corner of the sitting room and had run out of bobbin thread. She stood up to release the bobbin case ready to refill it. As she clicked it on to the spool winder, she knew, and smiled to herself.

Her rib cage never quite returned to its ante-natal days. Recently she had resorted to trying on her black crepe dress, bought when she went to Paris with her job. In the mid-seventies it had been expensive and she remembered buying it in a shop in Knightsbridge as an investment. She knew, when she bought it, how useful it would be and sure enough it had been until now. She was going for a Christmas meal and thought it would be perfect; quiet and not glitzy, but smart, special. Well there was no way that she was going to prise the zip closed, and disappointed, returned it to its flowery padded hanger and hung it back in the wardrobe.

A cotton skirt caught her eye in the children's section at the top of the escalator, such a pretty little summer skirt, soft primary colours, a real little girl skirt. She could see by the waist that it would fit. She longed to try it on but the fitting rooms were downstairs. She couldn't use the children's fitting rooms. It was good value, reduced in the sale. She wondered if the assistants would even allow her to try it on and protest, "No madam. It's a child's skirt." When would she wear it? She knew that she was really too old. Even the other day she tried on a silk voile top and skirt. She had seen it before, pretty and soft. She could see herself in it, all wispy and romantic. After much deliberating she decided against it. She found excuses. When would she wear it? Would she look too young and what about the shoes? She walked into town. The town was too small, the walk not long enough. Other women walked and like her, they were not shopping. She caught their eye and half smiled. She saw other people, who not so long ago looked middle aged, no age and now they walked with a stick, their hair grey, carrying a floppy shopping bag or worse still, pushing the formidable tartan 'Sholley', like a terrier, its wheels ready to snap and bite, tender skin grazed, drawing bright red blood, bringing tears to eyes. She took to noticing other couples, couples her own age, out shopping. They looked sexy. They would walk close, his arm around her shoulder, she would turn towards him, laughing, her hair dancing and moving. In the fitting room next to her a French woman was trying on a shirt. She was tall and wore red cord trousers, not new but slightly faded, comfortable. She would have worn them around the house, not shopping in the King's Road. She thought that she was bold to wear such brightness on a big arse, and admired her courage. She could see that they loved each other. She could see it in his eyes, undressing her, trying to help her decide but hindering instead. She liked being hindered, the foreplay. Getting him to undo her buttons, which she could have so easily done herself, flirting with him, her French voice warm and passionate. He said that she looked good, smiling and touching, making her feel special. Would they make it home before the climax? Not all husbands were so active. Hers would have been one of those. Most would sit outside the changing rooms on comfy sofas reading newspapers in a convivial sort of way, unable to share ordinary activities with their wives, no longer turned on and in tune with their sexual desires or come to that, their own emotions. Wives would peel off their clothes and flounce out of the fitting rooms in their never been worn dresses and spotted socks making excuses for the hairy legs. The husbands would look up from the paper, comment and turn the page to the sport, satisfied that they had contributed towards the purchase and could go home, flop in the chair and watch the telly. Even on a Saturday morning at seven thirty, couples were full of abandon, in a private world of their own. Reaching for the cornflakes, shamelessly he would feel her shape through the stretch denim. She would hook her thumb in his hip pocket as he pushed the shopping trolley. Sometimes couples would stop and kiss, not caring what other people thought. They would be wrapped against the cold in knotted scarves or wear sunglasses to shade and protect their love. They would sit, leaning towards each other sipping wine, intent.

Returning from maternity leave, Sabiha looked beautiful. She too was French and she looked stunning, absolutely radiant. She had not always thought of her in this way. Sometimes she looked tired and pissed off. Her clothes lacked attention, almost unkempt. Her translucent skin, open and bare, her long dark frenzied hair worn tightly back in a pony tail, scraped and pulled from her scalp, ready for business. She wore pale grey trousers, the crease sharp, boring into the pavement and carried a matching jacket over her arm. Her silver jewellery was discreet and caught her eye. Had she looked like that, chic and sensuous? She didn't think so. She didn't remember the compliment. She had always felt harassed, cooking meals and boiling nappies in a bucket on the stove. Sadly she didn't feel that anyone thought anything. Her mother had bought her a length of fabric; beige wool boucle. Out of it she made a skirt and waistcoat, fashionable at the time and felt fairly confident until she saw the photo. The colour didn't suit, it drained her fresh complexion, making her look grey and older than her years. About the same time her husband suggested buying her a new coat. For years she had been making her own and this was an invitation not to be missed. She saw herself wearing it in fifty years time, threadbare at the cuff, but still good. Sensible. Going for the camel she stood back to look in the mirror. Her husband held the hanger while she contemplated the reflection. It would have been a terrible mistake. Dull, dowdy, dough ball, dead. In sheer fright she chose a red wool velour, big and bold, thick and cuddly, a stark contrast to the classic belted camel, Swinging from the shoulders, it would be worn for ever.

She was kneeling down in the room where her children had lain, fast asleep in their bunks, having played and worn themselves out. Her youngest son was keen to show her what he had done. A jigsaw puzzle of beech woods occupied the whole wall opposite the window. She felt as though she were in the wood, deep and peaceful, the dense leafy canopy keeping it cool and dark, shafts of sunlight filtering through, puddles of brightness splashed on the spongy undergrowth. It wasn't stuck to the wall, it was suspended from the top outside edge. The woodland scene hung, each piece clinging, dependent on the piece above. It could have buckled and crumbled at any moment. The weight and tension was unbearable. She could see the wall behind where some pieces had come out. They lay face down on the carpet. Deftly, her son refitted them. The room was empty. She longed to return the stark white walls to sprawling flowers, make it hers again. She stood up and went out of the room. The landing belonged to the house where she had been a child. The stairs too, were partly from then and partly from her own house. She stopped. On the stairs there were three baby's matinee jackets and bonnets, new, discarded, their satin ribbons smooth and untied, the delicate knitting springy, the tiny mother of pearl buttons snuggling in the softness. Suddenly she was aware of a terrible thing. The banisters of her stairs had been ripped out, splinters and nails exposed, the plaster raw and gritty. There was nothing to hold on to. They lay in the hallway below, broken up. Where she had lived as a child had been totally demolished. Nothing was recognisable Utter devastation. No, no, no. " It's all right, it's all right."

She knew that her mother thought about those April mornings before her daughter was born. Jewels filled with promise. That precious special time when sleep would not come, feeling big and uncomfortable, frightened, the pillow damp from seeping tears, her lifestyle gone, wondering about the change that was about to occur. Lying in the stillness listening to the birds, their endless chatter, competing and calling, protecting and arguing, just like people really but harmless, just going about their business. The sun waiting to disperse the blurry light, the clear golden brightness pouring in across the bed, the air crisp and cool. Her birthday was special to her and she felt disappointed if it was forgotten or not acknowledged in some way. She sat beside her mother with a buoyant birthday energy, smiling and attentive. She wanted her mother to surprise her and forgive her for not buying a card.

"What day is it today?" she asked her mother.

"Why, it's Saturday." she replied "Bath day."

"What's the date today?" she continued, not giving up. Her mother pulled out Ethel's Daily Mail, which was stuffed down the side of the chair. She held it at arms length, her eyes peering to locate the date at the top of the page. Carefully, she read it out.

"Saturday 16th April 2006." A blank expression spread across her face. "What day is that?"

It was as if she had been forgotten and lost her place in her mother's time line.

"It's my birthday."

"Is it?" she said. That ended the conversation.

She hadn't noticed it before. For the last twenty years a sky rocket had obscured the view. It had grown too big and on windy days it built up enough momentum to demolish the screen wall. How it had not done so she put down to her husband's skill with cement. It was tall enough to be blown from all directions. The foot high sapling had been bought when her son was one, on a visit to the RHS garden in Wisley. Over the years it had provide shelter and fun and food for the birds, but on Sunday its darkness had been cut down. In the fuzzy grey Monday morning light when she opened the blind, she saw it perched high on the ridge tiles eating the waves from the satellites in outer space, regurgitating them and spitting them into programmes, sending them down the cables into Val's front room. The big patch of sky which had been there all the time was open and honest, no longer concealed. Each morning when she opened the kitchen blind she smiled to herself. Imagine seeing a fantastical prehistoric lyre bird just standing on the roof. She remembered seeing a picture of one in her big grey encyclopaedia; it was on the bottom right hand corner of the page. Like a lot of things, she never knew where that book went. She remembered once, when she was small that she had seen a brown bear in the woods. It was in the distance, just sitting very still, quietly contemplating. It was the very beech wood that hung in her dream. She didn't tell her sister of her fear. As they got closer, it was of course a massive rotting stump and she was glad that she had said nothing. Even now she still looks out for bears. The giraffe nodded her head agreeing with the zebra sitting next to her. Their hooves rested on the hand rail of the seat in front of them. She had seen this strange sight when she had been driving to work on the motorway on a sunny winter morning. The animals were sitting upstairs on the bus. Like her, the bus was at a standstill, snarled up in the traffic on a bridge spanning the motorway. Slowly as the traffic moved, the shadows changed and the animals disappeared.

She rolled over and stretched into the cool cotton corners of her bed, trying to remember. She was warm and liked the cold fresh feel where her heat had not penetrated. She lifted her arms out of the warmth and sandwiched them around her pillow. Like a mint in the mouth the hot pale skin was cooled and her soaring temperature restored. For years she had been plagued by hot flushes which started deep in the epicentre of her body and spread through her like a wave to the surface, disturbing her sleep, making her restless and wakeful. They happened in the day too, but in the public eye she just had to ignore them. If people noticed, which they did, she would just say that she did feel a bit hot and open the window temporarily. At night time, sleep did not return easily. She lay unsettled, her mind travelling through time, remembering. She lay supine, stretched out fully, her arms folded over her chest like stone carving on a coffin. Even though it would have been cooler, she did not open her legs or spread out her arms, partly because she didn't want to disturb her sleeping husband and partly because it wasn't her. Arms and legs had always or nearly always been close to her body, crossed or folded. She had a friend who always slept with her legs wide open, unable to sleep in the restricted confines of a sleeping bag without the zip fully undone. She was glad that she had experienced such abandonment.

In her forties her sexual appetite increased. She remembered returning from a Mediterranean holiday, sunned and golden, just burning with desire. She shared her body with her husband but if he was sound asleep or not there, she explored herself. She lay on her back and smoothed her hands over her naked body, feeling her ribs and the indentation of her waist, the loose papery skin of her stomach. It had never retained its firmness. Once, it had been taut like the skin of a ripe tomato before blanching, now it was the other way; thin like the skin after blanching, no fat, no flesh, just soft and pappy, wrinkly. No amount of sit ups reduced it. In fact, exercise just increased the firmness of the muscles and the skin just hung over like a muffin top. Although vexed, she didn't dwell. After all, she was usually clothed. Her hands spread down to her thighs, fingers denting the dimpled flesh then back to her breasts, her thumb and forefinger toyed with her nipples alerting desire, pulling and teasing, lingering. She rolled over on to her front and hauled herself on to her elbows. Her breasts hung free and even in the gloom she could see where the sun had not reached. She pulled at her tits, hard and firm, nipples like beads, excitement spread through her. She pulled her tits towards her mouth and explored the nipples with her tongue, licking. Inside her the frantic eruption, ten on the Richter scale was unstoppable. She flopped down on the bed. Between her thighs was wet and creamy. Writhing she held the cheeks of her arse apart, she pushed herself harder and harder into the bed until the throbbing, fluttering feeling subsided and ebbed away. She had first felt that feeling in her father's bed. Her child's body had responded. She had had no idea what was happening to her. Something deep inside had been aroused. Silently she was losing control, her internal muscles contracting, her body deciding what to do, like an animal. The pulsating confusion inside her made her feel frightened and disgusted with herself, yet strangely she liked the odd sensation; nerves were made to tingle and dance. Exhausted, and vibrating with desire, she went to the bathroom. Making herself feel insatiable was a new experience, and wonderful though it was, it didn't last. The nerve supplying the most sublime feeing was cut. It was almost inevitable that it would happen.

More than anything she wanted to be able to walk. She did not see her life ahead confined to a wheelchair, incontinent, needing help every time she moved, unable to use up her abundant energy. Her surgeon knew that. Life would not be worth living, not life as she wanted it to be. She first saw it on the MRI scan, when only a few hospitals in the country had the technology. The growth lay along her spinal cord for several inches, held fast by the tangle of nerves that supplied the lower part of her body, clinging and clawing, slowly spreading.

For years she hadn't known what it was that was causing the most horrendous pain in her leg. She ignored it until it became impossible. In hospital, long ago when her children were small, she felt like a hideous experiment. Still in the loft gathering black sooty dust was the plaster cast of her body, designed to keep her rigid. She was injected with dye and stretched on a rack, but she found that the worst thing of all was that she felt that she wasn't believed. Because she coped so well with her pain, she was not convincing. When all tests failed to throw up an answer she was sent to the Luing Cowley clinic. Of course she knew it wasn't psychosomatic. At last, she could request a second opinion and went off to Harley Street to see Mr Trotter. She had come by his name in a roundabout sort of way. Many years ago her godmother had worked as a nanny for a local G.P. and he suggested that Mr Trotter would be able to help, which of course he did. He knew immediately that it was a tumour and that summer, part of the insidious growth was removed. Each time, surgery proved more difficult, both for her and the doctors, and although the high risk remained the same, her last operation followed by a course of radiotherapy rendered that intense delicious pleasure, that twinkling night sky, a thing of the past. She was left feeling in limbo, unprepared, yearning for those feelings, recreating them in her mind but unable to feel them. Of course her husband still wanted her but she had no desire at all to participate. She could feel nothing physically and to her it seemed wrong just to give herself to him for his pleasure when there was nothing for her. It was like washing the dishes, a job, and that made her feel awful. Explaining was difficult. In a way she felt immoral, a bit like a whore servicing a client. She hadn't realised how she would miss the closeness and the passion shared with her husband. Her mind lurched back to those oppressive grey mornings in her father's bed. She felt disgusted and sordid at the thought. She remembered the floating scum on her wedding day. That feeling never left her, that feeling of being used, second hand, no longer perfect no longer complete. Not having any desire made her feel childlike and innocent. Painful memories surfaced and returned. They lurked, festering at the back of her mind, entangled like the tumour.

Her small son looked up at her. He was wearing a brown woollen coat buttoned up to the neck, his trousers were tucked into his red Wellington boots. She had made the coat out of one of her mother's, a very good Weatherall coat, completely reversible. All her children had worn it and it was known as the garden coat.

His left eyeball was loose and did not fit snugly, unlike his right eye it moved around in its socket. She reached towards his eye and removed the loose eyeball and the white stringy mucus that was causing the problem. He continued to watch her with one eye. The blank socket was a perfectly smooth hollow like a melon ball shaper. The eyeball the size of a marble, it was heavy and smooth. Carefully she slipped it back in position, his eyelid enclosed it, keeping it safe. Unperturbed, her son continued playing with his tractor.

It had changed from a shop that sold roller blinds to a Costa, its maroon trademark inviting you to sit and relax, even though you had a trolley load of shopping to put away. The door was closed. It was not time to open. Through the glass walls she could see a young man in matching maroon getting ready for the onslaught, checking the multi purpose coffee making machine, stacking mugs and cups neatly, arranging the linked-sales biscotti and tempting dreamy muffins by the till. The tables were already wiped with anti- bacterial spray, chairs neatly tucked under. There were two types of furniture; hefty tall wooden chairs with high round tables and spindly chairs with chrome tables, designed so that you did not outstay your welcome. Both were uncomfortable, scattered across the floorboards and in true Italian fashion some spilled outside, protected from passers by with a wrap around windbreak in spite of there being no wind. She could see that he was getting ready, concentrating. That time before opening was treasured, your thoughts could be your own. It was organised and ordered. Once the customers appeared, all that was gone. There would be noise and muddle and dirty dishes.

When she was fourteen she went to Skegness. It was not a place that her parents would have visited but her friend from school had moved there with her family. She had missed Sue. Her family was modern and ate yoghurt, spooned out of a family size pot into a bowl. They had benches at their table instead of chairs. Sue's mum and dad had bought a guest house, a rambling Victorian property in the town. It had three floors and two bathrooms. She and Sue used to wait on the guests and take their orders in a little red-covered jotter. Although there was an assortment of tables and chairs in the dining room, they had all been lacquered black and arranged so that couples and families felt private, not overheard. In the evenings the girls laid the tables ready for breakfast. She loved making it look nice, collecting the tablemats from the sideboard, laying the cutlery and folding the napkins. Even now, when she cooked a special meal or any meal, she liked looking and checking and arranging the table. It was satisfying, sometimes done hours in advance so that she could give it her time and consideration. It was very personal, and she rarely trusted anyone to do it as well as her or how she wanted it done.

Challenge made life interesting. It didn't have to be anything major. Her latest challenge was to be frugal and spend as little as possible for two weeks. She had become totally conditioned to spending over a hundred pounds a week in Tesco's. What made it worse was that she had seen programmes on T.V. showing what a raw deal a lettuce producer and a dairy farmer got from the big supermarkets and it incensed her. The weekly shop had become too much of a routine and far too expensive. She felt pressurized and bad if she didn't go, as though the world would end or she wouldn't have anything to eat which was absurd. She shopped locally, surviving on the basics and what had accumulated in the cupboard. She carried it precariously on the handlebars of her bike, carrier bags stretched and deformed with the weight. She would stop and talk to people in the high street, cluttering the pavement for those who wanted to get by in a hurry, and call good morning across the road and wave to familiar faces. It was certainly more sociable and much more economical. She was not tempted to fill her basket with unnecessary store cupboard items that would sit until the use by date rolled round in 2011. She was no longer tempted by the special-offers, buy two, get one free. It was either too bulky or too heavy so she didn't feel compelled to buy.

Driving into London was a challenge. Well driving anywhere was a challenge. But into London was even more so. It was something in her life that she never expected to do. Whenever possible she chose her time carefully, e.g. a Sunday morning at 5am. She checked the A-Z, so that she knew the route. Of course nobody wanted to see her that early on a Sunday morning so she had to go later in the day. She would brace herself for the onslaught. It was impossible to relax. The tension in her face was clearly visible. Her brow furrowed and her concentration fixed. Her eyes darted from mirror to mirror. Music was turned off in the very complicated junctions. Negotiating, what her son called the 'square-about' at Hanger Lane was particularly gruelling especially going north and so was Hyde Park Corner especially going south. She could hear the golden silence when she turned off the engine. She sat motionless, listening to the world going on around her. She had to prise her hands from the steering wheel and unfold her locked fingers. Exhausted, she would sleep, curled up on her son's bed or loll in a chair in an attempt to rid herself of the continuous vibrating whirr inside her head. Or even park in a lay-by or a service station and sleep. The other day when she was talking to her exam group, she compared the journey to starting the coursework, which, for the pupils was completing twenty sheets of A3 paper. Although it was daunting at first, taking a step at a time was her philosophy.

Finding Douglas was a challenge. She knew that she would not be able to settle until Douglas was found. She would not give in; she never did. She would try the British Red Cross. They might have a record of Freda Evans when she worked at Piper's Hill. Maybe one of the nurses in the photograph was Douglas's mother, even more reason to find him and return the picture. She would write to Mrs Lakin. Would she be able to remember those days sixty five years ago? The letter from the Red Cross returned promptly. Typed on headed paper it really only confirmed what she already knew. Piper's Hill was classed as a small auxiliary hospital with only thirty beds and patients stayed about twenty days. The curator also wrote that many records were destroyed as a matter of policy shortly after it was demobilised in 1947. She really hadn't expected a reply from Mrs Lakin. She had sent her letter via her brother's estate as she had no way of knowing where she lived. However, eventually she did receive her letter and there was the reply on the mat. Eagerly she opened it, this was truly primary research.

"I remember Sgt. Weir very well. He was in charge of discipline and if any of the patients misbehaved he reported them to me and brought them to the 'office' for interview. He was great to work with and I can't remember exactly when or why he left us." She remembered the name of one of the nurses in the photograph being Dolly Garrett and she remembered Freda "who did quite a bit of secretarial work for us" Coming by this information seemed remarkable.

Trying to piece together her father's whereabouts was proving elusive.

A new thing had appeared on the message tool bar or maybe she hadn't noticed it before and in frustration, clicked on it. Although it wasn't a 'trying to find' message board it was a finding out information board, much the same thing really. The turn over in pages was rapid and within a week her message had gone, so she wrote another, more cryptic. Messages and advice came thick and fast. There did seem to be a Brisbane connection. She typed in Douglas's mother's name and that was it. Her nieces Sue, Chris and Helen all contacted her. At last, a breakthrough. She was so excited, she could hardly contain herself, the missing family, the second family found in less than a year. She printed the information so that she could read it. Holding a piece of paper and reading it in black and white was proof and not likely to disappear or be deleted. She sent a lengthy email to Douglas, explaining all.

Douglas had not known his father. He only knew what his mother had told him and now he was not sure what to think. Douglas's first words were that their father was a 'conniving old bugger.' He had always assumed that 'their' father had been killed in an accident just after the war. His mother returned to Australia with him in September 1949 on board the Arcadia. He was three years old. She had obviously aroused his suspicion and she imagined him rooting about, looking for papers and documents to confirm this revelation that had intruded into his life. His mother had gone to the 'Mother Country' in 1934 when she was twenty five to work as a governess and tour Europe. 'Her passport was very busy, just like a modern day back packer.' Her passport had changed from her maiden name to her married name (her maiden name). After reading her email, Douglas had doubts about his father's marriage to his mother. He said that they went on a day trip to France and got married there, because of all the rules and

145

regulations imposed by the Church of England. Within days Douglas sent a family photograph and an unseen picture of her father in the full regalia, taken in 1938 and signed 'with love John xx,' obviously given to Dorothy, Douglas's mother. Now she had doubts.

They knew each other years before she had originally thought. Maybe they did get married. She printed the photo A4 size and showed it to her friend. She went all goose pimply. It was his eyes, she said. They follow you around, like the Mona Lisa's eyes. She was sure her friend had psychic powers. Other pictures followed, taken before the war. There was one of her father with Douglas's mother, posed for. She stood slightly in front of him, not touching. Was it their wedding photograph? Like Gordon said, he had a high opinion of himself. His neck was much thinner that she ever remembered. She hoped that his rough necked jacket buttoned right to his throat was hot and uncomfortable. His moustache was clipped neatly over his top lip. He looked smug and arrogant. His uniform was immaculate. Brass buttons gleamed. Did Dorothy clean his shoes on her hands and knees, buffing them up with a soft cloth? He loved himself. The photos made her feel hurt and angry; frustrated at the lack of trust. There were no photos in the brown leather case of her mother with him wearing the full regalia. Was she not good enough? Was Dorothy Lillian's life spoiled like her mother's? He preyed on women who were vulnerable, sweet talking, using them, taking advantage, taking things not his to take. Were Dorothy's dreams shattered when he abandoned her, leaving her to bring up their son on her own, leaving her to pick up the pieces? Did she feel like Margaret had felt when he upped and left, three years earlier, angry and bitter? If they were married, he was in fact a bigamist. If they were married, so was she. As, at the time of marrying James in 1975 her 'first' husband was very much alive, still married to his first wife, but also 'married' to his third. Her father's passport was dated from August '49. Did he plan to go with

146

Dorothy and Douglas? She would never know for certain. Then Douglas sent another photo. It had been sent from Dorrie, (his mother) to her sister Jean (Douglas's aunt) in 1947. It was a picture of Douglas in his pram. On the back of the photo it read. Douglas, John and I will be with you as soon as John is demobbed and we get our passage to Australia. Love from Dorrie. So he was going to go. Within a year he was with another woman, her mother. She felt sorry for Margaret and Dorothy and her mother and herself. They all paid the price.

Her father smoked. He always had. Weights and Woodbines were replaced with Players. In later years, still expected to buy presents, she would buy fifty Players in a presentation box and he would decant them into a slim leather cigarette case and offer them to all and sundry in the pub, flirting, making out he was generous. She knew that smoking killed; that was why she bought them. The Captain on the packaging guaranteed a pleasurable experience. Sure to kill. When he was no longer able to drive and get to the shops himself, her mother bought the cigarettes. "He has few pleasures," she would say. When the doctor called to see him, he advised him not to smoke and she never bought another cigarette. A heavy smoker for eighty years, it must have been tough on the withdrawal symptoms. Good. However, the cigarettes didn't kill him. He never got the punishment that he deserved.

She found a photo of herself as a child. Douglas's eldest son looked so like her at that age. The auburn hair and the shape of his face, the smile, teeth with gaps and the same fair complexion peppered with freckles.

Chris was into family history and also emailed interesting snippets. She was sure that Dorothy Lillian had married James Arron after her father and that the list of descendants where she had sourced her information was incorrect. She felt a family feud rising. Chris explained that her descendants were labourers, originally from

Eastbourne, not the toffee nosed lot from Lewes. Douglas confirmed Chris's suggestion. Dorothy Lillian had married James in 1975.

Her son showed her how to scan photos and send attachments. She sent the small square black and white photo of the boy she had assumed to be Douglas, the photo that had caused so much intrigue.

"My ears don't (didn't) stick out like that and I've never been allowed to have a short haircut like that."

Who was the boy with the sticking out ears?

Douglas was keen to feed her appetite for information and further emails and photos followed. The photo that interested her most was one of her father, a leaner, younger man, without the moustache. She had never seen his top lip without the clipped brush of coarse hair. Again he wore the full regalia. There were no such pictures to find when she and her sister had cleared their mother's house.

Until recently, she wondered if she should have had a photographer at her own wedding. Knowing what she knew now, however, she was glad that she had so few pictures. At the time she was not keen on having formal photos done and apart from that it had been too expensive. It would have been a mockery, her father pretending and lying. And now, if she had, he would be there, the centre of attention as he was at her sister's wedding. She would have thrown them away. She loathed him.

She had no way of telling as she approached her third age how she would fare. She had seen couples older than her change, just repeating things for the sake of it, without smiles, forever grumpy and off-hand with each other or complaining, not a good word to say or just plain quiet, yet with perfect strangers, lively, their conversation interesting their language colourful. Was that because they knew each other too well? Was there no longer anything to find out, to share and enjoy as they had fifty years earlier when just a walk down the lane was pure magic?

Already, there were changes. Her husband was becoming forgetful. In the kitchen she kept a small red bowl, once used for steamed puddings, for vegetable waste. As soon as there was anything in it her husband was off to the compost or filling a trench across the garden. Regardless of the weather he would go in his slippers ducking under the wisteria dripping with flowers, across the grass and disappear through the rose arch. He didn't bring the red bowl back. No, he had been deadheading and cutting back a clematis that had got a bit unruly and had totally forgotten about it. He called it slipper gardening. He was always coming up with quirky expressions and new words like the spoonerisms that rolled off his tongue like war cashing or cork phops. He made these changes as he spoke. She was slow to grasp. To her it was like deciphering code. He just thought it was funny. 'Don't forget your bag, Dad,' just had to be one of the silliest family quips that always brought a smile. He gave people nicknames like Gearbox and Loopy and Dogo and deliberately mispronounced words.

She had to admit that she was uncertain of spending the whole time with her husband, like being on holiday permanently which, normally she would look forward to. It took on a new meaning. Breathtaking scenery and good looks were not enough. Surely he would get on her nerves and he would easily get annoyed as he had the other day when she started to cut the grass, cutting in short lengths, doing it as she always had without a care in the world, just wanting some fresh air. He didn't say anything to her but she knew he was irritated. Hurt, she stopped cutting, left the mower standing in the middle of the grass. Leaving it unfinished, she went indoors. It didn't take much to irritate him, surely an aging sign. A helicopter flying low or a bike revving up would set him off, cursing and muttering under his breath. She learnt to ignore him. It was best to.

He knew every part of the canal between Slapton and Grove. He had been fishing there since he was a boy and could remember every detail, the time of year, the weather, who he had been with and what fish he had caught and what bait he had used. He could recall a particular patch of weed or the absence of a willow and how a heron had startled him when riding his bike on the towpath. There were signs displayed, advising not to fish because of the cables. He remembered fishing with a cane rod and even a stick when there would have been no danger of an electric shock and/or death. He used a straightened out safety pin for a hook. He never tired of telling her, and she always listened, quietly agreeing. It was a favourite haunt and had to visit at least once a year to put things in perspective. A warm, after the rain spring morning, was canal weather. She knew what he was thinking.

She liked hearing him laugh. He would laugh at things on T.V. She would be upstairs sorting the washing and hear him laughing in fits and starts. He didn't laugh for the sake of it or because he thought he ought to. When he laughed, it was genuine, an infectious, spontaneous laugh that made you sit up and take notice. He read books, all sorts of books, fact and fiction. McCarthy's Bar was a funny book and had him howling with laughter – unable to contain himself laughter, disturbing the peace and disturbing his wife on the white sands of Jumeira Beach. Often he only referred to a book, to check a plant name or the name of a bird, and he did not return them. Every librarian's nightmare, he would leave them in ones and twos on the table or open on the settee or even on the bookshelf, all skewwhiff.

He followed cricket and football, mainly on TV with the volume turned down to the minimum but also by going to matches. He did not suffer fools gladly and found the commentators too full of themselves, intolerant of their incessant verbal diarrhoea. He himself was very well informed and could remember matches from years ago, and like the in-depth knowledge of the canal could recall players and moves, goals and fallen wickets. He would be a useful team member in a pub quiz. He enjoyed the nostalgic pilgrimage to the Oval, finding it just as he remembered. Squeezing through the narrow turnstile and walking in, numb to the raging traffic outside the ground. The assurance that apart from the sponsor, nothing had changed. He didn't say anything, he didn't need to but she could sense his anticipation, his eagerness as they climbed the concrete steps to the stand, her husband just ahead, stopping at the top to take in the view, filing along a row of empty seats, keeping his eye on the wicket as he unfolded the tip up seat. He would scan the ground, just a handful of supporters, the ground staff brushing and rolling the hallowed tartan turf, the gasometer half empty, the prospect of play imminent, the tranquillity broken only with a distant siren or a plane passing over. For some time he had been frustrated with his team's performance and their lack of commitment and was anxious that, when the coin was tossed they made the right decision. She often went to cricket with her husband, partly because she liked the leisurely atmosphere and partly to hold his hand. He was not confident on the tube and did not want to get lost. Ahhhh. She had only been to two football matches with him, she was not keen and it was usually blowing a gale or freezing cold. So unlike cricket, the crowd packed in like sardines, the abuse hurtled at the players, the coaxing from the terraces, the oos and the ahhs and the noise when twenty five thousand fans leaped to their feet when his team scored. Years ago her husband's team had been very successful but for the past few seasons they were in decline, with her husband refusing to go ever again. Of course she knew he was just saying that. He would go back.

They had been planted about Easter. He had always enlisted a son to do the job saying that they were nearer the ground than him. This, however, was no longer the case, as all his sons were now taller than their father. More like, it had become a habit. The potatoes looked good, the tops still green and upright. In previous years they had seen them wilting and yellow, the stalk just above the ground slimy and already decomposing. Her husband was simply dying to see what they were like, even though it was a fortnight too soon. He took the fork and pressed it into the warm damp earth. There they lay, creamy white, the jewels in the crown. Carefully he lifted them and placed them in the riddle, rinsing them in the water butt to remove the loose soil still clinging to thin papery skin. The taste was exquisite. When her children were small they would find them in the earth like looking for treasure, collecting them in their buckets then wash them standing on a chair at the sink. Even potatoes the size of a pea were bagged, "I want that one mummy," finding it underneath all the others in the serving dish. Her husband had always grown vegetables. Growing onions had to be the most satisfying, grown from seed, not sets, that was not truly growing them from scratch, thinning them out once they started to form, lifting them in August, letting them dry off on a chicken mesh rack across the garden then rope them and hang them. The end of the summer. Over the years the vegetable garden had been reduced. "Remember when the redcurrants used to be there and the gooseberries used to be beside the fence." He would remember when the two of them would sit by the back door and shell peas when their babies were sound asleep. She remembered making jam and filling the big chest freezer in the garage with vegetables.

Sometimes his romantic longing annoyed her, at times he was moody and seemed to dwell on things. At the time he wasn't sentimental about the gooseberries, even on a day-to-day basis he did not strike her as being so, but when the time had passed the looking back seemed more important than or better than the present. With each year that passed the picture seemed rosier. She on the other hand did not have the same urge to reminisce. She wasn't so sure about them being the good old days, they were just the old days. The gooseberries had scratched her arms and made them bleed. The other day she had been demonstrating how to prepare a kiwi fruit for a fruit salad when a child had said that he didn't like the black seeds.

"Did you like kiwis when you were small Miss?"

"Good Lord." She replied. "We didn't have kiwi fruit, it was just after the war. We didn't have any fruit at all. You were lucky if you had an apple. People even ate the core."

He was always recapturing memories shared long ago proud to be able to tell and share momentous occasions. He would recall queuing to see Jimi Hendrix and it costing a guinea. Of course his sons had heard of Jimi Hendrix, one of the greatest guitar players of all time, but what was a guinea. The queue to get in was long, but they made it, unlike today, no tickets in advance, no phoning frantically and five minutes later, sold out. No, calm amicable queuing all the way to The Rifle Volunteer, the pub on the corner, where the tempting smell of hot dogs or rather the onions got the better of her. It was packed, the psychedelic patchwork hallucinating across the dance floor. Hendrix wore his hipsters, crushed purple velvet and tight, flaring out below the knee, leather Cuban heeled boots. His frilly satin shirt unbuttoned, his lithe body firm and brown gyrating to the beat thumping out of his electric guitar. Spellbound the crowd rocked mesmerized by the magic. His Afro hair framed his dark features and his mouth shaping the lyrics. Her husband said to his sons that they would be able to say that their mum and dad had seen Jimi Hendrix at the Cali and that had to be a wow factor. When she called her son, "Hey Joe." He would always reply, "Where are you going with that gun in your hand." He was called Joe.

He would recall the Sunday afternoon in 1966 when England won the world cup. They had watched the match together on a black and white T.V. saved up for by her mother. They sat on the settee in her parent's front room, her mother at work, and her father sitting where he always sat. She was sitting on his left and although the football was important, all he really wanted to do was give her a good snog. The pitch was all cut up from the horse trials the previous week and although it had rained in the morning it was a good afternoon. He could remember the match vividly, the two goals by Martin Peters and Geoff Hurst keeping the score equal at full time, the tension unbearable and the hero Geoff Hurst, scoring two further goals in extra time, sensational. Her husband had to contain his celebrations until the evening when the Cross Keys opened. Of course players today did not compare with the heroes of '66. He identified with the salt of the earth characters, he was passionate about the game.

Her brother in law explained to his grandson why one of the Russian dolls was missing.

"Well Michael," he said.

"When your Great Grandad died, he wanted some of his ashes taken back to his home. Some of the ashes were spooned out of the jar that sat on the shelf in the conservatory and put in the Russian doll and buried in Great, Great Grandmother's grave. That's why it is missing."

The bright Russian doll nestled in his mother's bag along with the sandwiches and thirty daffodil bulbs, a last minute purchase. His mother was a good woman, loyal and reliable, a worker and like many women, kept things together. She too had persevered and endured a lifetime and years of hardship with a man who like his contemporaries was a piss head. She herself had seen him beat their new dog with a tennis racquet, the first thing to hand, holding him by the scruff of the neck, the dog yelping and cowering and in a fit of rage one day he launched the ironing board straight out the door and into the fish pond. That was the sort of man he was and how she remembered him. Only in later years did he mellow. Dutifully until the end his wife was at his beck and call.

Her husband's father had died. She could have called him her father-in-law but she didn't go in for family titles. He was patriotic and it was his dying wish that his ashes were returned to 'his' country, to a graveyard on the edge of the Carpathian Mountains in the Ukraine. She could see where her husband had inherited his sentimental longing. Her husband, his mother and Bradley, his nephew, travelled back by coach. The long, long journey across Europe and Poland to the bus station in L'vov in the Ukraine took two days, travelling none stop. The bum-numbing experience frequently came back to haunt him. The toilet was soon full and didn't work and the young border guards were inhospitable, brandishing their Kalashnikovs, strutting about, deliberately making them wait and reading or making out that they were reading their passports and visas. Visiting the grave was the first job. A simple wooden cross, draped with a wreath indicated the grave. They stooped over the dry earth, the pink phlox gently swaying in the warm afternoon. Mykola, her husband's cousin, turned over the earth with a stunted rusty spade. Her mother-in-law buried her husband along with the bulbs, Mykola covered them with soil. Her husband's nephew looked on, wearing his panama hat, his face hidden. Minka, Mykola's wife wore a scarf. Her husband took the photos. In the photos, in spite of the age difference, they all looked the same. The splash of spring would appear year-after-year long after his father had been forgotten.

There was little friendliness. Her husband found the people mercenary. They would only do anything for money, preferably dollars, American dollars. Most of the men were consumed with alcohol. From morning till night they were drinking. The wives and mothers, their heads covered in flowery gypsy scarves, loosely tied under their chins, trying to make ends meet, making the most out of gherkins, peppers and melons. The photographs did not show smiling faces.

Looking back must be a 'getting old' thing, simply because there was more time to look back on than there was to look ahead to. Besides the regular year he was forever measuring time and kept a diary of important events, which sometimes proved useful if she needed to know a date. He marked time by his dental appointments or sowing the cabbages or getting the car tax and so the year became fragmented. He could look back in 1978 and see when the first daffodil flowered, He would record extremes in the weather or when he embarked on a particular project. The entry for Friday 26th January 1996 reads V. Cold, E wind, early bulbs coming up. When their children were born he would record their name and the time they were born and maybe the weather conditions.

His capacity to learn was amazing. Redundancy had forced him to rethink and he went on to study horticulture at a local college. Every week he had ten plant names in Latin to learn. And he did. They never left his side. The note pad would go everywhere; he would write them and re-write them over and over again. She never doubted that he would get ten out of ten every time. She knew he would, and came home on Friday evenings pleased with himself, then promptly started all over again with the next lot. She knew that she could not do that. Spellings on a Thursday morning at junior school were her greatest fear. She never remembered getting ten out of ten. A test or an exam of any sort brought her out in a nervous cold sweat. Her most recent test was her food hygiene certificate; even ticking the boxes was nerve racking. All the way through the training she concentrated, trying not to be distracted, listening to the teacher, trying to retain the information long enough to put the tick in the right column. As soon as it was over she escaped to what she knew. A month later her certificate came in the post.

Regrets, he kept under wraps. He was not good at keeping in touch. People slipped out of sight into the past. With very good intentions he would say that he would phone or call in, but he never did.

"Don't forget to pop in."

"Give us a call. You've got my number."

Time passed by too quickly, suddenly he had left it too long and it was too late. Her mother would have said, "A man of words and not of deeds is like a garden full of weeds."

Like his mother he was a worker, never off sick, good at his job, one of the best, head hunted even. But as he said, you got no thanks. He would say that you were only as good as your last shift, just a number, a cog in a wheel. He was a cynic. It annoyed her however, that he was so often right. He felt wasted, not proud of completing his working career, redundant, on the scrap heap and although he had a refreshing change of direction, he did not call that work, it wasn't the same and did not compare with the oil and grease of industry, the deafening machinery, the smell in his hair and black ink ingraining his hardworking hands.

He looked up at the cupboard that contained their random selection of glasses. "You've still got that vase" he remarked. Then looked at the rose arch. Stupidly she read his mind and thought that he was going to cut a rose and it would be on the table when she came home. Now, he rarely surprised her. On Christmas day, her sister would phone and she would ask her what she had had. She hadn't had anything from her husband – nothing to unwrap. Her sister,

157

always hard up, listed the latest must-have cook book, a natural sponge and a jewelled bag from Monsoon. The most perfect little luxuries sounded so inviting and so Christmassy, chosen with care and love. She had nothing to say, nothing to share and was glad when she had rung off. He hadn't always been so thoughtless, so cheeseparing and resistant to giving. She remembered presents and surprises but not for many years, like the little green box handed over while having lunch in a pub overlooking the hubbub of Covent Garden. She could tell that he loved giving her those earrings and sometimes wondered why he didn't make it more of a habit as it had given him so much pleasure.

***

Her discontent had been aroused when her sister phoned. It was the way she said Perpignan and Roussillon as though she was fluent in French, confident, which she was. Her sister had walked and eaten good food and seen vivid blue gentians and eagles soaring and had good weather and hadn't needed to book. The pang of envy. She felt almost joyous when she said that she had missed the ferry home due to an accident and the awful weather around Nantes. Good, at last she thought, something to spoil. At times she was an absolute cow, to think that she could think like that. Her sister described it vividly and made it sound so good, in perfect harmony with her husband, enjoying their holiday together. She herself had done that awe inspiring journey across Europe and seen the eagles. But the eagles her sister had seen sounded better than hers. She loved her sister and did not feel good about herself.

It had been a useless weekend, occasionally she had those. There were parts that were good. She had got her road tax and there hadn't been a queue, she had made two Maderia cakes, she had gone for a short walk with her husband. She had sat around too much, falling in and out of cricket, which her husband had set at mute because of the irritating commentators. She had laughed at Last of the Summer Wine, the three bikes careering down the road until of course the three of them fell off into the verge. Rain, heavy at times had soaked her washing and although it had eventually dried, she was disgruntled with the bother of it, looking at the sky, checking the cloud as if she could do anything about it. She had made Mediterranean cous-cous and coleslaw, enjoying the vegetable preparation, cutting it neatly and putting it into piles. The dreamy new potatoes sprinkled with dill. It had started on Friday evening, feeling pleased with herself, grass cut, supper half started. She did not really use that word. It was her sister's word for when the day was done and she cooked food for friends. It was her mother's word too. She would stand on the step ringing the bell from Benllech Bay, shaking it for all it was worth as her voice would not reach behind the garages. Dinner was for dinner time and supper was for supper time. She didn't do tea or lunch; must have been a Scottish thing. When her husband had reversed up the drive, the car did not sound good. Her husband walked in, thoroughly cheesed off.

Swathed in red, she stood proud and upright in the field where the cloud of locusts had descended and stripped her bean crop. Despair etched deep into her face, parched like the earth beneath her bare feet. How would she feed her family?

The L'Oreal advert came on, the sickly smooth chocolate lilt, "Because you're worth it." it rattled him, made him feel angry. "Tell that to the poor woman in Africa, trying her best to feed her family. She's got absolutely nothing." Trying to stay beautiful and keep the aging process at bay was the least of her problems.

He was grumpy all weekend. The weekend ended by cleaning the top of the cooker. It was truly awful, a disgrace. What would people think? She didn't even fry anything, yet it was splattered in grease, stuck fast. The thing was it wasn't just a couple of day's grease, more like a month. She felt much better.

He always said that he was not going to sit down and read the paper. Well, there was little chance of that as they rarely had a paper and if they did he sat at the kitchen table with it spread out in front of him scanning the sport pages, not really reading it. However he did do a fair amount of lounging around, but in front of the television, reading teletext and ceefax and even watching day time TV. There was more huffing and puffing and sighing. He blamed his dodgy knee for not going for a walk and going out had lessened dramatically. Even going fishing had lessened. Normal things, like levering himself up on his arms from the top step of the ladder to get into the loft was posing a problem and getting down was even worse. He stood in the dirty blackness in the clutter of aerials and tubs of Lego negotiating how to descend onto the top rung. When he first said about having difficulties in the loft she thought he had got stuck in the loft hatch because he was too fat. But no, he was just not so agile. She took these things as signs of getting old.

Yesterday he said that he had thought about her during the day. She asked him what he had thought. Like her, he found it difficult to express what he really wanted to say without it sounding glib. Words seemed to come out sounding insincere and superficial. He liked coming home. Coming home to her, always there, loyal and dependable. Whatever the day had thrown at her, always the same, in control, never fractious or moody. Standing quietly in the kitchen, slicing onions and squeezing garlic. She liked preparing vegetables and found it relaxing, therapeutic even, arranging them on the wooden chopping board, using the knife or her hand to push them into neat piles. She liked the sound of the knife cutting through them and the soft tap of it making contact with the wooden board. The subtle tints of roots banked against each other. Vegetables were more resilient than fruit. Fruit was juicy and had a mind of its own. It slipped off the board and needed containing and collecting on plates. Her hands became wet with the juice. Although she said hello, she did not take her eye off what she was doing, she would continue to stir a sauce, concentrating, waiting patiently for it to thicken. Sometimes he slipped his arms about her, he couldn't help himself. Her train of thought uninterrupted, she continued to stir. For whatever reason they no longer looked at each other, not really looked. They said their goodbyes and hellos but did not linger. She remembered platform 15. How could she have been so blind? They needed to look at each other. When his warm brown eyes met hers the two of them dissolved, there was a chemistry, a mental fascination, something so profound, something so deep and mysterious that it was hard to explain and she wasn't good at explaining. He said that nobody could have loved her like he did and she believed him. She knew that he loved her but not as he had when they had watched the World Cup in 1966. She too, felt affection, but agreed that their relationship had changed. It had changed from the head over heels frivolous love, which, in their youth, they thought was love, to a devoted, unconditional, never-ending love. She tended not to think about it. It was already in place. Although sometimes she thought she would like to be, she was not lovey-dovey and she did not sit next to her husband on the settee even though he asked her to.

They sat together quietly on the garden seat, a trug full of broad beans between them. The shells fresh with recent rain snapped open. Their thumbs pushed the beans from soft fibrous beds into a saucepan, the shells collected in the bucket beside their feet, bound for the compost.

Her zest for life was never far away. Life was too short. All too soon it could come crashing down. She lived life to the full, not wasting precious energy on things that she could do nothing about, not worrying about things beyond her control.

She wanted to do something exciting like live abroad, not to holiday but to live, to see if she could. For some bizarre reason she wanted to go back to that dusty hillside town and walk the narrow streets, empty by day but alive in the evening when the heat of the sun had finally gone. It would be warm and balmy even when sudden rain washed the streets, and thunder storms threatened power supplies. She wanted to go to the bakers in her flip flops and sit in the shade and sit outside in the rain. Getting used to it would be a challenge, learning the language would be a challenge. But she wanted it all, she didn't want to give up what she had known, what she felt safe with, the house and the garden where her children had grown up. She was torn, half of her was optimistic and couldn't wait to go and the other half thought she was mad.

In the summer months she had taken to bat watching, taking her drink and her rug outside if it was cool and sit patiently for the birds to stop chirping to each other. On the long summer evenings they would not stop roosting until after ten, like naughty children who would not settle. Then she would wait, staring up at the space increasingly sharpening in the twilight. Her eyes wide and unblinking, she tried to encompass the whole sky, slowly scanning from left to right. Trees and plants became black as the light changed, roofs were huge against the silver sky. Through wispy cloud, half a moon blurred and fuzzy cast a doubtful light. Always a surprise, she would see one or sometimes two, their black velvet quietness and sudden darting movements silhouetted and gone. She would miss those moments if she went.

She went back for a number of reasons. Firstly, to see if she could, because she had never been abroad on her own before, secondly, to experience how it really was, to see if she could cope with the intense heat, the flies and the

162

barking dogs and thirdly, she wanted to see if she felt the same as she had done two years earlier.

She smelled of Spain. It was a heavy concoction of deodorants, cigarettes, sweat and nervous energy, a sweet sickly smell. A smell of travelling. Where it touched her neck, her hair was wet and she knew it smelled like a dog's coat caught in the rain. Rivulets of sweat ran down her back and soaked into her black top. Drifts of salt appeared where it dried. Her skin was damp and clammy. Waiting in the wrong queue, waiting in the right queue and getting tickets, missing the train and waiting again, getting off at the wrong stop and waiting again, getting on the wrong train, getting off, getting on the right train. She soon understood why young people needed a year to do their travelling. In the night it had been immensely hot. Airless. The shutters and windows were closed to keep out the heat and the mosquitoes. She slept in snatches, remembering nothing of her dreams. Ants, half the size of the ones that heaved out a pile of sand at her back door at home, were everywhere. Without her glasses she could barely see them, but she knew they were there, running about, going about their business on her pyjamas and in her hair, carrying away flakes of skin from her itchy scalp and nipping her legs. She longed to open the window and adjust the shutters, but the arrangement looked complicated and she might have made too much noise. Slowly a grey light filtered through the shutters.

***

She was comfortable in the cool air-conditioned taxi and directed the driver where to go. She had been too late for the morning train directly from Barcelona and settled instead for the nearest small town, taking a taxi from there for the last few miles. The dusty godforsaken town was desolate, just as she remembered. It was so familiar, past the shop where she had bought a Daily Telegraph for the cricket reports on the Test Match or a Daily Mail, where the man spoke a smattering of English. Having a newspaper was comforting, when everyone around spoke in foreign tongues. Years ago newspapers would arrive days late, if at all. Technology now, however, enabled the paper to be printed every night, in Europe at least. At a price. She remembered, when her children were small, having a paper delivered, just in case an adult had a conversation with her and she needed to know about worldly issues. It didn't last long. She grudged throwing the paper away, unopened and unread. When they were on holiday, her husband would read snippets to her and she would listen and give him suitable replies. He would read the headlines and they would comment on global warming or obesity or bank charges. To exercise their minds they would do the quick crossword. They shared possible answers and would resort to the dictionary when their minds failed. Eagerly, they would check their answers the next day. Along with the travelling iron, the dictionary was a holiday essential. She never went away without it.

Past the bar where she and her husband first sat. The lady, the same lady wiped the dust from the round chrome tables, busying herself, waiting for customers. There was nobody refreshing themselves, having a 'shampoo' or a coffee. The car turned right and then left through the narrow streets. She found *esperar* in the back of her phrase book and showed it to the driver. After the cool comfort of the car, the dense afternoon heat, the suffocating cotton wool heat pressed against her, sapping her energy. She knocked frantically on the back door where she had been so glad to leave. There was no reply. Catching the eye of the driver, sitting with the engine running, she said she would try the front door. Using her arms to indicate where she was going, she disappeared along the back of the garages, down a few steps and into *Carrer Iglesia*. There was no reply. She returned to the car. They both muttered and shrugged their shoulders. They drove slowly, past the phone box, where she had phoned home, tears streaming down her cheeks, hardly able to speak, a lump in her throat, putting on a brave face, trying to sound cheerful, feeding the machine with euros, lying, saying she was fine and the weather was hot, deeply sad, hearing the voices from home pressed close to her ear and then in mid sentence, bleep, and they were gone. Past the bench where she had written post cards to her mother, lying, saying that she was having a lovely time and that the weather continued to be hot. Past the bar where the locals came out to play, shaking off the heat of the day, talking and laughing, playing *boule*. She asked the driver to drop her off at *la estacion*. She waited in the sweltering dusty heat for the train back to Barcelona.

Feeling pleased with herself, she reflected. She had travelled abroad alone and felt reasonably safe and confident. Sometimes she felt apprehensive, but mainly her trip had been exciting. She had revisited Riba-roja d'Ebre and although she hadn't been able to walk around as she would of liked, she could feel the emotions flooding back. Whether she could live somewhere so hot with the ants and the barking dogs, in a culture that was quite different, she couldn't decide. She would have to go back again.

Her son sat on the favourite chair at the kitchen table, sipping his hot tea noisily. She stood beside him gently moving the palm of her hand in small circles over his shoulder. Through the softness of his jumper his shoulders were lean and bony. She said "Goodbye and take care, especially when you are on your bike." He stood up and wrapped his arms around his mother. Against him, she felt small. "I love you." She said, squeezing him towards her as she had done when he was small.

"I love you too, mum."

"I know you do." She replied.

She wasn't sentimental about her children leaving home. That was for other people, people who cooed over babies in prams. Growing up was inevitable. She saw it as moving on and being independent. She did not dish out her feelings and say 'love you' on the phone as she had heard mothers say when they talked to their children. And although probably true, it sounded insincere and an afterthought. She knew that people wondered if she was experiencing 'the leaving the nest syndrome' just as they wondered if she had missed not having a daughter. She was fiercely possessive about her sons. No. She did not miss having a daughter.

Joan emailed. She was mastering her new lap top and had to wait until the New Year to enrol for classes. It was over a year since she had met Gordon with his soft patient eyes and Joan, his wife. She wanted to visit again, now that she had had time to think. To ask questions before it was too late. It would have to be soon. She went alone with only the radio for company. She listened to 'On your Farm' and Sunday Worship from Birmingham Cathedral celebrating One World Week and the omnibus edition of The Archers, 'an every day story of country folk.' Still going strong. And Kirsty Young playing Ronnie Corbett's Desert Island Discs as she drove along the M9 towards Stirling. She never did hear his last two records.

Her teeth sank into Joan's friendly, homemade buttered tea bread. She sat next to Gordon on the settee, exactly where she had sat a year earlier. Gordon's brother and sister had joined them. They mulled over their father's pithy life. Mildred leaned forward in her chair.

"He used to call me lantern face." She said, stroking her chin. "And he used to steal buns from the bakers."

Gordon remembered his father taking him to camp and singing when he had had a few too many. He had not shown his children the back of his hand. Jack had been a long distance lorry driver and many times had thought to stop in Leamington Spa, a place name that was familiar. He also said that he thought their father had gone to Australia.

Someone must have known his whereabouts. She would never know. Connie showed her siblings photos of their father. "Oh aye." He had not been part of their lives for so long, they were used to living without him. Memories were tired and faded. There was little to glean about her father. Joan took a photo of Connie with Gordon, Mildred and Jack. The good thing to come out of the brown leather case was that all the children were in contact and their children would know how it was.

Carried on the damp autumn air the full time whistle blew. It was quarter to five. How would she feel when she was on her own, like her neighbour, suddenly bereaved? She had been at the line collecting the washing, folding it neatly and placing it in the basket, ready for ironing when the whistle blew. She remembered watching her husband playing football, her feet cold, waiting for the end, the final whistle.